# A BREATH OF SCANDAL

# S ANNE GARDNER

## ALSO BY S ANNE GARDNER

### SINGLE STORIES

An Affair of Love

The Very Thought of You

Till There was You

Absolution

Cold and Lonely, Lovely work of Art

For the Love of a Woman


### Poetry

In the Silence of the Unspoken

# A BREATH OF SCANDAL

# S ANNE GARDNER

Affinity
Rainbow Publications

2023

A Breath of Scandal
© 2023
By S Anne Gardner

Affinity E-Book Press NZ LTD.
Canterbury, New Zealand

Edition First (1st)

ISBN: 978-1-99-104048-0 (paperback)

Editor: Angela Koenig
Proof Editor: Lisa M
Cover Design: Irish Dragon Designs
Production Design: Affinity Publication Services

## ACKNOWLEDGMENTS

As always, I want to thank Julie who has been a constant support from the beginning. She pushed me, was patient with me, and held me to task. Thank you, Julie. You truly made this book happen.

Thank you to all the loves of my life, my wife and our children. Without them the world would have no meaning, no music, and no colors. They are everything.

Eternal love to the two little girls that reign in my heart; K and T, you brought me all the old sweet memories of long ago.

And finally, to my dearest friend Mel; I miss you every day. You were a constant encouragement, and you always found the words to bring me back to my writing.

To my readers, thank you for your patience and waiting for this book. Thank you.

# DEDICATION

To my love, you are the constant, the sun and the moon but more than all that you are the heart and the blood that pumps it.

*Ti amo tesoro mio, mi bella amada, Lisa*

# TABLE OF CONTENTS

# CHAPTER ONE

"If you think you are taking my daughter away from me then you don't know me very well," Adele said in controlled anger. She clenched her hands into fists as she tried to control her emotion.

"I am not taking her away from you, you have to believe that." Gillian tried to reassure her. "She loves you; I would never do that, Dell." She took a step closer to Adele as she said this.

"Will you move back to New York?" Adele only wanted those facts.

"No."

"Then consider this the last time I deal with you. My lawyers won't be as generous," Adele said, seething with anger as she took a step closer to Gillian.

1

"Adele, don't do this," Gillian begged.

"She's my daughter!"

"Not according to the law!" Gillian regretted the words as soon as they left her mouth.

Adele flew at her with all the anger that she had controlled only moments before. She grabbed Gillian by the arms and began to shake her hard.

"I'll kill you!" Adele spat as she shoved the younger woman against the wall violently.

Upon hearing the commotion, Gillian's parents ran into the room and were appalled at the scene that was unfolding in front of them.

Brian Kendell stepped in front of Adele Visconti, preventing her from having access to his daughter; Gillian slid down the wall and was sobbing on the floor as her mother went to see if she was all right.

"What do you think you're doing?" He demanded. Never in his wildest dreams would he have ever thought that the woman in front of him would be capable of doing what he had just witnessed. "Get out, Adele, leave now!"

Marilyn Kendell helped Gillian up off the floor. "Are you alright honey?"

Gillian nodded as she gradually stood up with her mother's help as her sobbing continued.

†

Adele stood still as if in a daze. Her eyes were focused on the woman that had, in a single sentence, destroyed her world a week before. Adele was processing what she had just done and, to her surprise, it hurt her more than it gave her pleasure. Gillian was destroying her life; why wasn't the love she felt for the woman dying within her?

Gillian was leaving her for someone else. She had fallen in love, her note had said, but worst of all, she had also taken their daughter with her. The child that they had shared together from the very first moment of conception to the actual birth; they had shared it all. It was too much to take and all the reasons in the world would not stop Adele from getting what she needed back.

"Adele, please go. I don't want to involve the police. You're a reasonable woman. I have grown to know you these past few years. This is not the way. Please, Adele, go," Brian insisted. "I am not going to allow this treatment of my daughter."

Adele was oblivious to all except the eyes of the woman that stared back at her now. The woman that had taken her heart and promised to treasure it. The woman that had, only a week before, coldly left her, leaving only a note behind, taking their child with her. In that short time, Adele had become the woman she had been all those years before meeting Gillian; and that was the woman that faced them all now. Nothing could have prepared them with what was going to follow.

"One last chance, Gillian," Adele said softly.

†

Gillian knew this voice very well. Adele, at that moment, she realized, was completely lost to her. She could not reach her no matter what her reasons were to be. Adele was beyond rational thought and the whole situation, for the first time in her life perhaps, was simply beyond her control or comprehension.

"You can see her whenever you like. I won't keep her from you." Gillian had tears running down her face. "Please Dell…"

"I live in New York!" Adele yelled losing her control once more.

"Please, why not try to resolve this peacefully?" Brian intervened again.

"Peacefully?" Adele stared at him incredulously. "That time passed when she packed up and left with our daughter, leaving me a 'Dear Adele' note. Isn't that what you Americans call it?"

Gillian's head went down as she was unable to look at the distraught woman in front of her. Adele could not stop the tears from falling freely from her eyes. Gillian noticed that she had lost weight and her face showed the deep lines of strain. The beautiful face of the woman that had been her world seemed tired; Adele had obviously not been sleeping.

Gillian wanted to just walk away. She didn't want to see the proud woman she had loved all these years falling to pieces in front of her, because, if no one else could tell, she could.

The once-proud Contessa de Caravagio who had wooed and pursued her, had truly fallen in love and love was now killing her. Adele was dying inside, and she could see it. Gillian turned away and tried to shut out the vision. She had to be strong and stand firm. Adele would survive, Gillian kept telling herself over and over again. It was for the best in the long run. Making a clean cut was best for all of them.

"Adele, sometimes people fall out of love. We can't always control what we feel." Brian was angry after seeing what had transpired when he and his wife had walked in. A part of him was glad that this union had come to an end for his daughter, but he also knew that a woman like Adele Visconti was better placated then egged on. He knew his daughter enough to know that her new friend would not last either. Maybe then Gillian would forget all this and settle down in a proper marriage. His daughter would finally, for once and for all, be normal again.

†

Adele turned to him, and her eyes became sharp knives. She had seen through him years ago and now her aversion needed no curtain. Brian took a step back from her and she smiled. She then turned toward Gillian again.

5

"Where is she? Or is it he?" Adele looked from father to daughter. "Where is this new love of yours?" She asked sarcastically.

Gillian wouldn't meet her eyes.

"Who is it!" She demanded again loudly.

Gillian visibly jumped as she looked at Adele now. "Candice," she murmured softly.

Adele's face registered her surprise. She took a step back letting the information register in her brain. Her disbelief showed in her face as she looked back at Gillian.

"Candice, the woman that…" Adele was still in disbelief.

Candice Wentz had been the woman that Gillian had been with when Adele first met her. The betrayal had become suddenly all the more encompassing and cruel. Gillian was leaving her for her former lover.

The space between them suddenly became unfathomable.

"Have you slept with her?" Adele asked soberly but softly. The only sign of what asking that question had cost her was the pounding she began to hear in her own ears and the way her right hand began to tremble.

†

Gillian noticed Adele trying to hide it. It would have gone unnoticed by anyone that had not known and loved her.

She closed her eyes as she answered the question, not wanting to see the reaction of the woman that stood in front of her waiting.

"Yes," Gillian finally answered softly. In that instant she knew that Adele Visconti would never take her back.

"I'll see you in court." Adele's voice was cold and distant. She pulled a cell phone out of her pocket and pushed a button. "Do it," was all she said as she closed it and put it back in her pocket. A malignant smile covered her beautiful face.

At that moment Gillian knew fear.

"Possession is nine tenths of the law. You can do as you like, but you are not keeping my child." Adele turned around and began to walk towards the door.

"Adele, what have you done?" Gillian was suddenly more nervous.

Brian and Marilyn looked at one another in confusion.

"Adele! Wait!" Gillian caught up with her, grabbed her arm, and turned her around.

Adele roughly pulled her arm away. "Don't touch me," she said menacingly.

"I don't want to hurt you, Dell," Gillian began as tears ran down her face.

"Don't call me that!" She growled back.

"I'm sorry." Gillian looked deeply into her eyes. "Give me my baby back, Dell," Gillian pleaded softly as she placed her hand on Adele's arm, more gently this time. "I need her."

†

Adele was unable to control herself from taking a step closer. Everything inside her wanted to take Gillian into her arms and love her. But Gillian wasn't hers anymore.

"No," Adele responded softly. But then she coldly added, "She's mine."

"I know she is but she's mine too. She's all I have. Don't take her from me, Dell, I beg you." Gillian was still trying to reach the woman that once could deny her nothing.

"You think I am going to give you my child after what you've done to me?" Adele asked in disbelief. For a moment Gillian could see the strain of her emotions begin to show in Adele's face.

Then what Gillian never thought would happen did.

"Come back, Gillian." Adele suddenly relented and her eyes showed the pain her soul was feeling. "Come back, I beg you." Her face showed the strain that she was experiencing. Adele was begging and Adele never begged for anything.

†

With an intake of breath Gillian stared at her in disbelief. Adele was begging her to come back. Adele Visconti was begging, her pride forgotten, and her arrogance laid at Gillian's feet. At that moment, more than any other, Gillian knew the extent of the love felt by the woman in front of her. So many times, and in so many ways, Adele had defied all for her. By her will alone she had taken her and not only married her but had given her a child. Adele had denied her nothing. But never in her wildest dreams did she ever think to see the proud and arrogant woman she knew as Adele Visconti Contessa de Caravagio begging her to come back to her, especially after she had told her that she had been with Candice. Realizing all this, Gillian felt the pain inside her grow twofold.

"I can't." Gillian turned away sadly.

Adele stared at her for a moment then walked out without saying a word, leaving Gillian behind.

†

She wasn't sure how she had been able to walk. Adele just kept telling herself to put one foot in front of the other and move. The whole world could have disappeared and she would not have noticed. A feeling of great loneliness and an aching that she knew would never be filled suddenly flooded her chest; she wished only to close her eyes and just make her life stop.

Gillian had left her.

The tall dark-haired woman went into the black limousine waiting for her and, when she felt the car begin to move, she let her head fall back and allowed herself to close her eyes. She wanted the world to stop turning on its axis. How could she live with this unbearable pain? Adele had been able from birth taught to control her emotions and her actions. She had learned from the cradle that some things were just not shown, and yet when she met Gillian, everything inside her had changed. All of her loved Gillian and now all of her was crashing with the unbearable pain she was feeling at losing her.

How had it all gone bad? Why? Why had Gillian stopped loving her? She hadn't slept in three days and now she felt the weight of the world pressing, closing in around her. When she felt the darkness take her she didn't fight it. She longed to lose herself into the abyss. And as so many other times in the last week, the past never released her.

# CHAPTER TWO

---

*"Paolo, why am I here?"* Contessa Adele Visconti de Caravagio *asked haughtily.*

*"It won't be long. You can present the cup and leave, Contessa. They know that you are on a tight schedule." Paolo Morenza, one of her VPs for public relations in the United States, assured her.*

*"Paolo, only ten more minutes, I'm leaving for Firenze in two hours." She told him impatiently.*

She hated these things, but she knew that as the head of Caravagio Wineries and the Visconti Estates, this was expected. She was the sponsor of these games and although she hated attending functions such as these, she accepted that she must. Adele was looking around, bored, when a

11

*young woman on the other side of the field caught her eye. Her mouth smiled slightly; perhaps the day would not be a total loss after all.*

†

The car made a sudden stop, and her eyes flew open. She looked around in confusion.

"I'm sorry Contessa, the car in front of us just stopped," the chauffeur apologized quickly.

Adele nodded and looked out the window. She had not been able to stop Gillian invading almost every moment of her thoughts since she had left her. She could not stop the thoughts of Gillian invading every second since this nightmare that she was in began. Suddenly the confines of the car were more than she could take.

"Pull over, please just pull over." Her voice sounded strained when she spoke. The chauffeur looked at the rear-view mirror and pulled over to the curb as quickly as possible.

†

He wasn't sure what was happening. He had been driving the tall dark-haired woman for a few days now. She was easily the most attractive woman he had ever met. Her dark hair in contrast with her fair skin was arresting. The

Contessa was tall and statuesque. There was something akin to magnetism that was mesmerizing in her arresting beauty. The woman exuded grace and her bearing was that of a proud individual. Authority exuded every pore and yet there was this vulnerability that escaped those eyes when she wasn't looking. Something very grave was obviously happening, that much was obvious in her semblance and in her speech.

As soon as the car pulled over to the curb, Adele pushed the door open and was barely out of the car when her stomach lost all its contents. She stood against the car for a few minutes afterwards and breathed deeply before getting back in again.

"Contessa?" The chauffeur's voice was laced with concern.

"Take me to the airport," she said, getting back in the car as one hand covered her eyes.

He drove her to a private hanger that he had been given the address to earlier by one of the Contessa's assistants, and as he arrived, he saw another black limousine waiting near a private jet.

When the Contessa got out of the car, he saw people get out of the other car as well. Two men and a woman holding a young child approached the Contessa. She took the small child, held her tightly to her, and then walked towards the waiting jet.

†

"Gillian! Gillian!" Candice ran into the house hysterically.

Gillian looked up from the sofa.

Candice only stared at Gillian. How could she tell her? How could she tell a mother that her child had been taken away under her very eyes? "Gillian…"

"I know, Candice," Gillian answered wearily. She ran her fingers through her hair and just let her head fall back.

"I called the police from my cell phone. They should be here soon," Candice said softly. "I'm so sorry, Gilly. I should have done something, but I couldn't…she had the gall to notify me," she trailed off, unable to find the right words.

"No one can stop her. She will never give her back." Gillian's voice was filled with such sadness that it broke Candice's heart with its resignation. "It's not your fault. Adele is beyond reasoning right now."

"We will fight her, Gilly. We'll get your daughter back," Candice said gently, trying to console her as she slowly walked closer and sat beside her.

Gillian smiled and her head came up as her eyes looked deeply into Candice's. "Adele will do whatever it takes. She doesn't lose."

"I know that better than anyone," Candice responded sarcastically. She immediately realized that her response was not right for the moment. "I'm sorry. That was uncalled for," she apologized.

"It's all right, Candice. I'm so sorry I hurt you."

"Gilly, that doesn't matter anymore." Candice took her hand and squeezed it. "What should we do, Gilly? I think we should call a lawyer. I know a good one that practices family law and is well versed with international issues if necessary."

Gillian smiled, got up, and walked out of the room without saying a word. They didn't understand. She knew better than anyone that no one who fought Adele ever won.

Brian had heard some of the conversation and saw as his daughter had sadly left the room.

"Brian, I think we should contact an attorney." Candice stood up to face Gillian's father.

"I agree."

†

Gillian called the police, explaining that the child was missing. She realized that with Adele all must be done with caution and great care. As futile as this act was, she had to try; trying was all that was left to her. In the end though, a part of her knew.

†

"Mother?" Giancarlo Visconti walked into the library of their New York estate apprehensively a few hours later.

"Carlo, I didn't know you were home." Adele got up and walked over to him, kissing him on the cheek.

Giancarlo searched his mother's face knowing only too well what he was about to hear.

"She's… Gillian's gone," Adele said softly. She walked away towards the fireplace that she had been standing next to when he had walked into the room only a moment before. "She's left."

"I'm sorry." He wasn't sure what else to say.

She turned towards him again as she searched his sad face. "She talked to you, didn't she?"

"Yes, she told me she was leaving," he said sadly to his mother.

Adele stared at her son, not knowing exactly how to discuss this with him. "What did she say to you?"

"She was crying and said that she would always love me, but she had to go. She told me to take care of you. What happened? I thought you two were happy. What will happen with Catty?" Giancarlo searched his mother's face. He had so many questions and that he didn't know exactly how to ask.

"Kateryna is here and here she will remain," Adele said with conviction and turned back to the fireplace.

Giancarlo wasn't sure just what that meant. He had been only twelve when Gillian had come into his life. They had been a family for four years. He had at first resented her for taking what little of his mother he had until he realized that, with Gillian's coming, he had more of Adele in the past four years than ever before in his life. Gillian had made them a family. She had been good for them both. Two years before, his little sister had been born. He loved his sister more than he could have ever thought possible. They had all been so happy. It could not have been more perfect. Why? Why had it all changed and what would happen now?

†

Gillian had been sitting on her old bed without moving after she had spoken with the police. Her head felt heavy, and the back of her neck hurt. She didn't think she could cry any more than she had for the past ten days. She looked around at what had been once upon a time her bedroom. So much had happened since she last lived here. The two most significant events were meeting Adele and having their daughter.

So much happiness all compacted in but a few years only to end up with so much pain. It would be so easy to just end it all, but what kind of message would that leave her children, because she thought of Giancarlo as hers, too.

Her child, Catty…

†

*"Breathe, Gillian, breathe,"* Dr. de Lapandusa encouraged.

"I can't... Oh!" Gillian was beside herself with pain. "Where is she? Dell!" she screamed again. It had all happened so fast. Her water broke and the contractions came quickly, one after the other.

†

*At that very same moment a dark-haired woman entered the hospital followed by three men and met by two others.*

*"Contessa, per favore, this way."* One of the men that met her in the lobby, guided her as he related all that had been set up for her. *"We have set aside this elevator for you."*

*She neither acknowledged him nor ignored him. She was used to his kind. It was always the same, an act of kindness she would ultimately get the bill for. This would be no different. That, however, did not matter now. She was glad for the assistance. She would be glad to pay for the courtesy later.*

*When the doors to the elevator finally opened up, she had to contain herself so as not to run. Adele had literally walked out of a board meeting, gotten on a jet, and was on her way to the woman that was bearing their child. Nothing and no one could have kept her away.*

*As soon as she entered the delivery room, her whole semblance of aloofness changed. Her features softened as she approached the woman who smiled at her.*

*"It's about time, Contessa," Gillian said with a smile.*

*"The entourage, always keeping me away, tesoro," she joked back. It had always been a standing joke between them since they had met. Adele took her hand softly and kissed it. "I'm sorry I'm late." This time her eyes were serious.*

*"The important thing is that you are here—oh God, here it comes again!" Gillian held on tightly to Adele's hand.*

*Adele looked horrified at the doctor. "Do something!" she begged.*

*"Okay Gillian, let's get this baby born. Push, Gillian, push now." The doctor encouraged Gillian.*

*"Oh!!!!!"*

*"Come on, Gillian, you can do it, cara mia, just push," Adele encouraged her.*

*"I see the head, Gillian; push hard so that this baby can enter the world." Dr. de Lapandusa smiled and looked back down again. "Here it comes."*

*Gillian screamed and clung to Adele's hand for dear life. A few seconds later the room was filled with the cries of their daughter, Kateryna Kendell Visconti. Kendell had been added for Gillian's beloved grandmother whom she had loved deeply.*

Adele stared at the child, unable to believe how one human being could be so perfect. The birth of her son had been a difficult one, and in the end she had been sedated. This was so different. The whole experience of seeing the birth had left her in awe. The beauty of her daughter left her, for once in her life, speechless. The doctor turned to her and handed her the child wrapped in a white blanket.

"Here is your daughter, Contessa." He smiled at Adele.

She looked down at the little human she held in her arms and her eyes filled with tears. Adele walked over to Gillian, handed her the baby, and locked eyes with the woman she obviously adored.

Gillian held her baby as she smiled at her and cried at the same time. She counted the fingers and the toes and thought her to be the most beautiful little girl she had ever seen. Adele leaned down and kissed her temple tenderly.

Gillian looked up at Adele. "She's perfect."

"Yes, she is, cara mia. She's perfect." Adele smiled with adoration at the infant in Gillian's arms.

"She looks like you," Gillian said dreamily and suddenly she began to look drowsy.

"She looks like us." Adele smiled and caressed her face. "Gillian..."

"Yes, my love?" Gillian looked up at Adele again.

"Thank you for my daughter. I love you, Gillian." Adele said, not caring who heard her. At that moment, the *outside world that she never exposed herself to just didn't exist. Gillian smiled, and all she felt were soft lips on her own before she closed her eyes to well-deserved sleep.*

# CHAPTER THREE

Gillian caressed her stomach as the tears continued to fall. "I'm sorry, little one. Please forgive me." She began to sob as she wrapped her arms around her abdomen protectively. "I'm sorry." She could not control the sobs that followed.

Candice walked into the room and immediately sat next to her and took her in her arms.

"I'm right here, babe. A day at a time, okay?" Candice said as she kissed the golden hair of the woman in her arms while she tried to control her own emotions. "Let me talk to her, Gillian, I can make her understand."

"No!" Gillian got up suddenly. "She would never let me go. It has to be this way," Gillian said as she sat down again. "She must never ever know about this child inside me, never."

Candice remained silent for a while as they sat side by side. She hated asking but decisions had to be made and quickly. "Have you thought about…?" she trailed off as soon as she saw the expression on Gillian's eyes.

"Yes," she answered then added, "There really is no choice." Her face took on an expression of longing that almost broke Candice's heart as she saw the woman she loved touch her stomach again. "I'm having an abortion."

"Gillian…" she said softly, not sure what to say to her.

"It's best. I can't bring a child into this suffering. Not to this." She ran her fingers through her hair. "This is my choice."

Candice looked at her and thought that never had she seen Gillian look so defeated. She had always been full of life and sunshine. The world always smiled on her, and the sun shone just to delight her. When Candice had lost her to the infamous Contessa Visconti de Caravagio, she thought her world would end. This was her chance to be with Gillian and nothing this time would get in the way of that. She hated how it had come about, but she would be with Gillian for as long as life would allow.

"I talked to your father. We both think you should contact an attorney."

"No, if I have a chance of getting Catty back at all, it won't be that way." Gillian sounded even more tired if that was possible. "You don't know what she is capable of."

"Gillian, she is not untouchable. We can do this. Catty is your daughter." Candice tried to control her frustration. "You need that little girl."

"Adele is not just anyone. She has not only the money but the type of power that makes her exactly that, untouchable. And she knows it. Catty is an Italian citizen. And like me she bares Adele's name. That alone in Italy would take time to disentangle." Gillian turned to Candice in desperation. "I can't wait that long, Candice. I can't! It might take years."

"Okay, okay, Gillian. I want you to get some rest now. You need it. We will fix it all sweetheart." Candice caressed her hair gently. Gillian seemed so fragile that it broke her heart to look at her.

"I know what I have to do." Gillian got up and picked up the telephone that was resting on her nightstand. Adele was waiting. She knew this as surely as she knew that nothing would ever be the same again.

Gillian waited patiently as the telephone rang while the woman on the other end longed to answer it.

†

Candice held her breath. Somehow, some things never changed. From the very first moment that Adele entered their lives, Candice had never known any peace. She had a chance with Gillian now and this time she would play the game to win by any means necessary. Adele would not get her way this time. She was best for Gillian. Adele had been only a momentary aberration.

"Hello?" Adele had been obviously waiting.

"I'm coming back to New York," Gillian said simply.

Candice stood up quickly but remained silent. She could hear the intake of breath from the woman on the other end of the telephone.

"Dell, I will move back to New York if that is what it will take. I won't take her away, Dell, I promise. She's your daughter, too," Gillian said softly. "It would just have been easier if I were here."

"Easier for who?" Adele asked sarcastically.

"Dell, I... I never wanted to hurt you. Please, Dell." Gillian's voice began to shake.

"It's not that simple anymore," Adele said coldly. The anger and betrayal she felt would not allow her to act any other way.

"How is she?" Gillian asked softly.

†

Adele had expected demands and recrimination but not that question; nor did she expect the distress in Gillian's voice to touch her as it did still.

"She's having her bath."

"I have the dolphin she loves to play with." Gillian tried to muffle the sob that escaped.

Adele said nothing. She knew that Gillian was crying, she could hear it, and she shut her eyes again attempting to dispel her need to comfort the woman that still was deeply rooted inside her. Adele was about to relent when she heard Candice speak in the background.

"Gillian, please sit down, sweetheart," Candice said with concern evident in her voice, trying to help her to sit.

"Adele?" Gillian began to say.

"No! I went to you, Gillian. If you want to talk, you must come to me!"

The line went dead.

†

Gillian put down the telephone gently and sat.

"I'll go to New York with you," Candice offered.

"No, I've already involved you enough." Gillian took a deep breath. She turned toward Candice. "I'm sorry, Candice; I'm sorry I involved you."

"Don't be silly. I will always be there for you and for Catty," she said reassuringly as she placed her hand over Gillian's.

"She asked me if we had slept together. I should never have answered that question."

Candice waited and she searched Gillian's face.

"I was scared. I knew that if I said yes... I thought Adele's pride would not allow her to take me back." Gillian looked suddenly sadder and closed her eyes. Her mind tortured her with the words that she never thought she would ever hear Adele say. *'Come back, Gillian'* Adele's plea had almost broken her heart.

Gillian's eyes flew open, and she stared at Candice.

"I don't know how she will react. I'm sorry. I should have thought of what that might mean to you." Gillian looked at Candice with concern.

"It's okay don't worry. I told you that I would be always there for you no matter what and I meant it. We are in this together," Candice said again reassuringly. "You aren't alone, Gillie, I'm with you every step of the way."

"Thank you, Candice." Gillian smiled and kissed her on the cheek.

"Let's get ready to take the earliest flight."

†

Adele pressed the end button on her cell phone and closed her eyes. When she opened them again all the anger and frustration inside her was visible.

"You are not taking my daughter, Gillian," Adele said between her teeth. "I'll be damned if I allow it."

At that moment there was a light knock on the library door.

"Entre."

The door opened and in walked a young woman with a child in her arms.

"Mia piccolina, come to *mama*." Adele stretched out her arms and the little girl hugged her enthusiastically.

The young woman then left as Adele dismissed her with a nod.

"How is my beautiful *principessa*? Adele said lovingly as she sat in a nearby chair, placing the child on her lap.

"Bath. I had a bath." The little girl giggled as Adele tickled her. "Mama, no!" she squealed happily.

Adele pressed her closer to her and kissed her dark curls.

"Where Mommy?" the child asked.

Adele's eyes filled suddenly with tears. Such little time, she thought. Such little time. She took a deep breath trying to control her emotions.

"Mommy is visiting your grandmother and grandfather. She will be home tomorrow," Adele said softly as she caressed her daughter.

"'Kay."

"Want me to read you your bedtime story tonight?" Adele asked lovingly.

"I want Punzel!" the child said demandingly.

"What?"

†

Brian looked up as he saw Candice walk into the kitchen. "How is she?"

"She's resting. We couldn't get a flight out till tomorrow morning," Candice said, visibly tired as she sat next to Brian.

"What?"

"We're going to New York in the morning."

"Why? We should call the police. This is kidnapping." Brian was getting more agitated by the minute and was visibly upset as he stood up. "Who does that woman think she is?"

"I tried to talk to Gillian, but she thinks this is the best way. I don't trust that woman but perhaps Gillian is right."

Brian looked at her then sat down again. "What's going on, Candice?"

29

"Gillian thinks that Adele might take Catty out of the country."

"Oh, dear lord," Brian said in exasperation.

Marilyn then walked in. "Where is Gillian?"

"She's resting. She's all worn out," Candice answered.

"What's wrong, Brian?" Marilyn asked, noticing the forlorn expression on her husband's face.

"Candice was telling me that Adele might be taking Catty out of the country."

"Oh, no." Marilyn became distraught and sat down next to her husband.

"We are going to New York in the morning to talk to her," Candice added quickly. "I thought we should call the police, but I'm not sure now. Gillian might be right. Let's see what happens when we talk to her. I know one thing for sure, this is going to be a hell of a fight."

Marilyn and Brian looked at each other as he placed his hand over hers, trying to give her strength in view of the situation. He had hardly seen his daughter since she had been with the infamous Contessa. At first, he had had to deal with his daughter being the favourite topic of the tabloid rag newspapers, and being stared at every time he and Marilyn went out. They had actually had to call the police once in the first two years to keep the sleazy reporters and photographers from blocking their driveway. It had all been so humiliating. Their neighbours stared at them and once they had even been asked horrible, humiliating questions as they were leaving their church. Their daughter's sexuality was something that they had kept quiet until it seemed that that was all that people talked about. The tabloids were merciless, the *'Contessa and the American'* had been the flavour of the week more than once with the local media.

It was at this time that Brian had found out more than he would have ever wanted to know of the woman his daughter had chosen to be with. Every detail of the woman's life had been dragged out for public consumption and the news was all bad. In those first few months, he was horrified every time a photograph of his daughter would appear yet again in one of the newspapers at the supermarket. At least now his daughter had come to her senses. God had finally made her see the light. One day at a time, he would get his perfect little girl back.

## CHAPTER FOUR

---

Gillian had closed her eyes and the world of memories invaded her mind.

*"Hi." She heard a soft voice say.*

*Gillian turned around and locked eyes with a beautiful set of dark eyes. She felt the pull of them almost instantly. She searched the face that she had spotted looking at her from the other side of the field minutes before.*

*"Hi," Gillian responded, smiling.*

*"Do you like polo?" the dark-haired woman asked seductively with a rather interesting accent.*

*"This is the first time I've come."*

*"Well, then you must see it properly. Come with me."*

*Adele took her by the hand and began to walk away.*

*Expecting no resistance, she looked surprised as she felt a pull and stopped to stare at the woman whom she had walked to the other side of the field to meet. Gillian looked at her for a moment before smiling.*

*"Okay," Gillian said, signalling the status quo was broken as she heard something inside her telling her to go.*

*Adele smiled back feeling an almost childlike joy for some reason. "You won't regret it, I promise you."*

*Adele stayed most of the afternoon and even participated with stepping down the pivots during the half.*

†

Adele placed her sleeping daughter on the ornate antique bed. Such an extravagance Gillian had thought when they purchased it. But their daughter only deserved the best, Adele had argued, and Gillian had relented.

Adele stood next to the bed now and looked around the magical enchanted room with murals of bedtime-story themes and fairy tales. All had been picked by both of them with such love. They had chosen every piece of furniture together like the carved bed that had the shape of a swan, and in the middle their daughter was nestled. Had she been too demanding, not open enough? Was it so wrong to give them all that her money could buy? Could she have loved her any more? Had she done too much? Perhaps she had not done enough? The questions continued to plague her since her heart refused to let go. She kissed her daughter on the forehead and opened an adjoining door and walked into her own rooms.

Gillian had wanted the baby close by when she was born. Adele had been surprised. It was not something she was used to but then Gillian had changed her whole life. She was more part of it all with Gillian in their lives. Being with Gillian, she had become a part of a real family and their children had been a major part of that. No longer was she alone or even lonely. Even while being away, for one business trip or another, she felt a connection with home that she had never experienced in her whole life. Gillian had made her feel and want for the first time in her life, and she had done it so slowly and effortlessly. How could Adele go back to that state of nothingness? The prospect of the coldness cut at her soul, and she wept silent tears.

Adele stared at the bed that they had shared together, and she knew that she would never be able to sleep in it again. Now her tears were those of anger and betrayal. She started tearing the sheets off the bed and began breaking everything in her vicinity. She knocked the lamps to the floor, and shattered lamps of French porcelain became pieces that covered the floor. With one swipe all the glass perfume decanters went flying and she continued the raging frenzy until the room lay in shambles with furniture turned over, and now, she finally stopped as she looked around her at the chaos. All was in pieces like her life was now.

She finally just went down on her knees and wrapping her arms around herself, she wept tears of such anguish that she thought her heart would finally truly break and die.

†

Gillian smiled in her sleep as she slept for the first time in days. Even in her sleep her thoughts would not leave the person that had had such an impact on her life.

*"This is incredible,"* *Gillian said as she leaned over the box watching the polo match.*

*"I'm glad that you are pleased, cara. Are you hungry?" She pointed to the silver covered dishes to the side with two people standing behind them waiting to serve the food.*

*Gillian walked up to Adele and whispered, "Should we be here?"*

*"I don't understand, cara?" Adele seemed confused by the question.*

*Gillian smiled. She was about to speak when two men and a woman dressed in elegant, dark, expensive Italian designer suits walked into the room and approached them.*

*"Contessa, they are preparing for the presentation and your limousine is by the stands to take you to the airport immediately after, as per your request," the woman said as she checked her agenda.*

Adele looked back at Gillian and spoke without breaking eye contact. "I won't be leaving early after all, Clare. Notify the airport. Would you like to bestow the cup to the winner with me?" Adele asked Gillian who just stared dreamily in surprise.

"Who are you?" Gillian asked in giddy fascination.

"I'm not sure right this minute. Perhaps if I keep you wondering a little longer you will have dinner with me, yes?"

"I...I can't," Gillian said, still not able to break their connection. There was an undeniable attraction from the very first moment when she had noticed Adele from across the field.

"All of you go. I will meet you at the stands in ten minutes." She dismissed them then turned her attention to Gillian again.

Gillian stared at Adele, not able to understand any of it, and yet she couldn't control her fascination for the elegant dark-haired woman that stood before her.

"I...want to spend some time with you," Adele said charmingly. "What must I do to make that happen?"

"I'm with someone," Gillian said, looking away quickly. Visions of Candice made her take a step back suddenly and turn away from Adele.

Adele walked up behind her and turned her around. "That will not do, cara. There can only be me," she said as her mouth came down, covering the lips that were beckoning. Their first kiss had been the most eye-opening experience in *all of Gillian's life. It was not only the taste of them but even the sound of the kiss that had her mesmerized. The kiss had taken life not only with taste but with sounds that had completely taken her by surprise.*

*Gillian's arms came up and her hands were filled suddenly with the dark mane of the woman pressing so intimately against her. She felt herself falling into a void that she could not fathom escaping.*

*Adele's hands could not pull her close enough. Never had she experienced such raw passion for anyone in her life. This woman already had a hold on her that no one had ever been able to attain. Gillian desperately realized at that moment that it would always be this way. Coming to that realization she pulled away quickly, setting Adele at arm's length.*

*They both stared at one another in surprise and wonder. "I can't do this. I don't want to…" Gillian became distraught suddenly and tried to pull away. "I've given my word to someone."*

*"Cara, this is unexpected to me as well," Adele said as she took a step closer. "Dinner…have dinner with me." Adele was serious. "I…want to get to know you."*

*Gillian walked away from her. "I'd better go."*

*"This is only begun, cara," Adele said as Gillian turned to her from the door.*

*"It cannot go anywhere from here." Gillian averted her eyes.*

*"So, you say," replied Adele with a seductive smile as Gillian looked up, challenge in her eyes.*

*"Yes, I say," Gillian said as she walked out the door.*

†

The next morning Adele walked into her library and took the call that she had been expecting from her overseas attorney.

"Giuseppe, *que*?"

"Contessa, leave the country. I have made discreet inquiries, and all is in place for you to get full custody of your daughter. They will not be able to touch you from here. I can start making the arrangements immediately. I can assure you full custody of your daughter here. The United States will reciprocate with Italian law."

"No. Wait for my call." She hung up the phone and sat down, closing her eyes.

Cutting all ties with Gillian was something she wasn't ready for yet. She ran her fingers through her hair feeling a weariness take hold inside her that she had never experienced in her life. What would this do to Gillian? And why should she care what it did to her or not?

At that moment the telephone rang again but this time it was her private number.

"Hello."

"Adele, I just got in. Can we talk now? I can be there in about an hour." Gillian's voice filled her whole being.

"Yes, come," she said softly, feeling every word cutting at her soul.

"No entourage?" Gillian said softly.

"No, just you and me." Adele tried to control the longing in her voice.

"Will you let me see her?" Gillian pleaded controlling her own emotions.

"Come." Adele hung up the telephone. She had to be strong, she told herself, over and over again. She had to be strong in front of Gillian.

✝

*"What's this all about, Gillian?" Candice demanded standing in the middle of the room.*

*Gillian looked back at her in frustration. "I don't understand it..."*

*"Why does she keep doing this?" Candice spread her arms all around the room. Their apartment had been filled with every flower imaginable.*

*"Candice, I have told her that I am not interested," Gillian insisted. She looked all around the room in frustration. Adele was like a storm that she could not control.*

*"Well, maybe you haven't really been blunt enough!"* Candice growled. *"She seems to be everywhere that you are and even when I am with you!"*

*"Don't you dare insinuate anything. I have not encouraged her."* Gillian was beginning to lose her temper in face of the accusation.

*"I don't want you talking to her, do you understand?"* Candice suddenly demanded.

*"Excuse me?"*

*"You heard me. Stay away from her. I have asked around and she is trouble."*

Gillian stared at her in disbelief. *"You have asked around? I told you I would not see her. I can't control what she does, but you should trust me."*

Candice just stared at her and then walked out slamming the door behind her. Gillian took a deep breath in exasperation. At that moment the telephone rang, and she walked over to the coffee table and picked it up.

*"Hello?"*

*"Hello, cara mia. Do you like the flowers?"* Adele asked softly.

*"Why are you doing this? I am with someone; I have told you,"* Gillian said, voice filled with apprehension. Every time she thought of Adele her body was flooded with the emotions she experienced during that single kiss they had shared. She shut her eyes, hoping to be able to shut out the

woman that produced those feelings in her. She felt guilty enough not having told Candice about it. They had met accidentally often, and Gillian could not lie to herself and say that she had not enjoyed it. There was something about Adele that attracted her. There was this constant raw sensuality between them that she had begun to feel, and she could not deny.

"I can't stay away, cara, I have tried. Truly I have. I need to see you," Adele insisted.

"No, I can't," Gillian said faintly, trying to control the fact that she wanted to see her, too.

"Why?"

"I have a partner. I can't." Gillian was feeling her resolve waver as she heard and felt Adele's pleading begin to take hold inside her.

"No entourage, cara, just you and me. I need to see if this is only a moment and nothing more. I cannot stop thinking about you. I think you are thinking about me as well, no?" Adele's melodic voice was like a magical chant that was melting all her defenses. "Come,cara, show me that I mean nothing to you, and I will just walk away."

"Adele, please…" she pleaded.

"No, I cannot lie to you. I know I won't be able to breathe until I take you in my arms again and allow my mouth to kiss yours. I am burning for you, cara mia. I have never wanted like this before." Adele's voice filled all her senses.

*"Adele, I can't do this," Gillian said in almost a plea.*

*"Come, just walk out of your door and I will be there. Come, cara," Adele coaxed, and Gillian's eyes shut as she hung up the phone with the last piece of resistance she had inside her.*

†

*Adele put the phone down gently. She looked out the car window saying nothing. A few minutes later she instructed the chauffeur to drive away. Since the moment she had met Gillian her emotions had been put on overdrive. From that very first moment she saw her she knew, and as much as she tried, she could not fight the ever-growing attraction inside her.*

*'How could she not feel it?' Adele kept asking herself over and over again. 'She's mine. I know that she is mine. How can she not want me! How can she not want me?' And this last thought, perhaps, was the hardest of all for her to understand. How could something that, for the first time in her life felt so right be wrong? Gillian had to love her. She just had to.*

†

"Will she see us?" Candice asked, unable to contain the nervousness in her voice.

"She is waiting for me," Gillian said as she picked up her overnight bag.

"No! You are not going alone. I don't trust her." Candice grabbed Gillian by the arms and turned her to face her. "No!"

Gillian stared into her eyes for a moment without saying anything. "I'll be fine," Gillian said gently as she pulled away and caressed Candice's face.

"No! You are not going alone," Candice insisted. She was not taking a chance of them being alone ever again. She did not believe Gillian's resolve. Adele was too strong.

"Adele may be capable of a lot of things, but she won't hurt me." Gillian tried to reassure her.

"You told me yourself that she is totally unpredictable. Did you think she was capable of abducting your daughter?"

"Catty is her daughter, too." Gillian saw the hurt register immediately in Candice's eyes. "I'm sorry, but that is the truth."

"I know that, Gillian…I know that too well."

Candice could not stop the pain from being evident in her voice. Catty should have been their daughter. Candice had told herself that many times for the past week. Every time she saw Gillian with the little girl, every word that Gillian said to her, every time she held her, kissed her, fed her, there was so much love in every look that she gave her child, every time a part of Candace was jealous. And Catty herself was so special. It had been so hard for Candace to look at the child and not see Adele in her features. Even there Adele had left her mark. Catty had her mother's blue eyes, but her beautiful dark hair was all Adele's. How could she have made even that happen?

Candice hated Adele; that she did not have any doubt about. She hated the fact that Gillian would forever be marked by the woman that even now was able to rule their lives. Even Gillian's daughter would forever tie them together. Candice hated Adele for taking away the only woman she had ever loved and for whom she would give her life. Adele would never get another chance. Gillian was back in her life now and there is where she would stay until the end.

Gillian looked down for a moment, took a deep breath, and faced the sullen woman in front of her.

"If you come it will be too much for her. She is too proud. If our separation becomes public, it will be a feeding frenzy. I have to get to her before that." Gillian tried to explain.

"What do you mean?" Candice asked in confusion.

"Adele is news. She burned a lot of bridges making our relationship public. I don't think she truly realized the connotations in the beginning. It was treated as a scandal of incredible magnitude in Italy. The paparazzi followed us night and day." Gillian spoke wearily remembering. "Her cousin even challenged her position on the board and came

close to winning. And through it all she remained firm…"
Gillian's voice trailed off sadly. "She will never forgive me."
She finished in a distant way that left no doubt.

"She stood firm…" Candice had to give Adele credit
for that. She remembered the times as well. She also
remembered the embarrassment and her own humiliation.

"Through it all, her brother was the only one in her
family that stood by her," Gillian said remembering back on
those days. "It was also hard on Carlo."

"Carlo?" Candice asked surprised.

"Our…her son," Gillian answered sadly. "I'm doing
the right thing." Gillian looked at Candice for confirmation.

"We will do this together. If it's New York then New
York it shall be," Candice said trying to reassure her. "It will
be okay Gilly, it will be okay."

"I can't ask you to just pull up…"

"You aren't asking. I want to do this." Candice
grabbed her hand and squeezed it.

"I can't let you do that, Candice," Gillian insisted.

"This is what I want."

†

*"Oh my God…" Gillian said covering her mouth in
shock as she was reading the newspaper.*

*"No cara, give me that." Adele tried taking the
newspaper away from her.*

*Adele had walked into the room and as soon she saw Gillian's face she knew.*

*"How long has this been going on? My God, Dell, my parents might read this!" Gillian was horrified. She paced around the room nervously then suddenly sat down in a nearby chair.*

*"I'm sorry, cara, I wanted to protect you from all this."*

*"Is this why we are suddenly taking this trip?" Gillian had been thrilled at Adele's suggestion that she, Gillian, and Carlo take a few months and travel to get to know each other in different surroundings. Gillian had loved the opportunity to build some bridges with the moody young man.*

*Adele's silence answered her question. Gillian got up and began pacing the room again.*

*"Tesoro…" Adele said softly.*

*Gillian suddenly stopped and turned to face her. "Is it true?"*

*"True? What?" Adele was evading and they both knew it.*

*"It is."*

*"Gillian…" Adele closed the distance between them and took Gillian in her arms.*

*"Oh my God, it's true! You could lose your birthright over me too." Gillian began crying.*

46

*"Listen to me..."* Adele held her at arm's length, forcing Gillian to look into her eyes. *"Nothing...I repeat, nothing is more important to me than you and Carlo. I won't lose, Gillian. I won't. I don't lose!"*

Gillian went back into her arms. *"How could they say such horrible things?"*

*"I'm sorry, Cara,"* Adele said as she held the woman she loved. *"I'm so sorry you had to find it all out this way. After tomorrow they won't have access to us at all."*

*"How could they do this? Our photographs...what about Carlo?"* She pulled away horrified.

*"I just had him picked up early from school. He should be arriving any minute. We'll talk to him,"* Adele said reassuringly. *"Unfortunately..."* Her face saddened. *"Carlo is used to the gossip and the tabloids... but this is..."*

*"This is true, about us,"* Gillian said sadly as she caressed Adele's face softly. *"All the rest, Dell...how could they print such lies?"*

*"You are the one good thing, Gillian... The rest...it's all true, cara."* Adele turned her face away in shame. *"All of it... It's all true. All they say that I've done in the past is true. All the affairs, all the questionable business deals, the drinking, the whoring... it's all true."* Adele finished, taking a few steps away from her. She looked ashamed to the point where she avoided facing her. The usual confident steps seemed to be unsure, like the woman that was taking them.

*Gillian stared at the woman in front of her for a moment in confusion. Then her love saw beyond what others saw and she beheld the shame and the pain that came with regret. Gillian put her arms around Adele and held her as the Contessa began to weep.*

*"I never wanted...never wanted Carlo to know all this."*

*"It doesn't matter. It's not you...not anymore," Gillian whispered in her ear and tightened her embrace. "This is another life, Dell, another life. It's only Carlo, you, and me. Nothing else will matter. He loves you so...and I love you, Dell."*

†

The buzzer on her phone broke into Adele's memories, bringing her back to the reality of her present.

Adele covered her face for a moment then pressed the insistent button.

*"Pronto."*

"Contessa, Mrs. Visconti has just passed the front gate."

"Thank you, Michael."

Gillian was here, she told herself. She stood up and looked out the palatial window, which overlooked the front steps that led up to the house. She stared as a car pulled up.

Her longing instantly intensifying as Gillian got out of the car and approached the house.

†

As if summoned by something greater than herself, Gillian's gaze went straight to the window that Adele was staring out of and, for an instant, both stood frozen in a connection that would soon be severed forever.

†

Adele stepped away from the window breaking eye contact first, and as soon as she did, she closed her eyes in pain. She braced herself for the onslaught she knew was forthcoming. Control, she had to stay in control, she repeatedly told herself.

†

Gillian walked into the house that had been home for the last few years of her life. She climbed up the twenty steps required even before entering into what they called the anteroom. She looked around, feeling detached from it. Was Catty upstairs where the bedrooms were or had Adele already taken her out of the country? She went in slowly as if in slow motion. Gillian entered the large anteroom and was again taken aback by the luxury of it. When she came for the first time, she had felt like a child staring in awe at the beauty of its length and height. The walls were covered in paper that appeared to be creamy damask silk. The lacquered antique pieces of furniture and the tapestries on the walls were only surpassed by the twenty-foot ceilings that had clearly been created so as to impress and impress they did. It all simply took your breath away. Your eyes feasted on each new discovery. Gillian took a few steps towards the long staircase but she was halted by the sound of the library door being opened to her side.

Adele stepped out and stared at her coldly. "Nothing for you upstairs…only the bedrooms. And that is no longer of interest to you." The venom in Adele's voice shook her to the very core.

Gillian seemed frozen, unable to move as she stared back at the woman whose countenance was cold and unyielding. This was a part of Adele she had never known.

"Come…" Adele said as she turned around and walked back into the room.

When Gillian walked into the library, she quickly found Adele with her back to her staring out the window.

"Close the door," Adele instructed without turning towards her.

Gillian took a few steps back and closed the door behind her.

Adele suddenly turned and faced her.

"Lock it!" she demanded.

Gillian stared at her for a moment, unable to move. Adele was pushing her, and she knew it. She wanted to see how far she could push. Gillian had seen her do it many times, however she had never been on the receiving end. Gillian turned again and proceeded to lock the door.

"Now it's just you and me, *cara mia*, as it should always have been," Adele said under her breath. She saw Gillian's hand tremble and smiled with satisfaction.

Gillian raised her chin as she turned to face her.

"Dell, where is our baby?" Gillian asked simply as her eyes suddenly filled with tears. "Please, Dell…"

Adele said nothing as she continued to stare at her.

"When did you get tired of me?"

"What?"

"When?" Adele began to pace. "Was it two months ago? One month ago? Or two weeks ago when we made love before I had to travel?" Adele stared at her now as she stood facing her.

"Dell…" Gillian said softly. "Please…"

"When!" she yelled, as her hand slammed hard on the table closest to her.

Gillian jumped at the sound.

They both said nothing as one waited and the other felt her life ending.

"Dell, where is Catty?" Gillian asked softly. "Please let me see her."

"I won't let you take my daughter." Adele's response was one of sadness, suddenly the ire completely drained from her body.

"I won't do that, I promise." Gillian took a step closer.

"You also promised to love me forever and always." Adele looked deeply into her eyes. "Why? What did I do to make you stop loving me?" Tears ran down her face unchecked.

Gillian thought her heart would break from the strain. "I don't want to hurt you anymore than I already have, Dell, please."

"You had me like no one ever has. I really believed you." Adele's face showed disgust. "I believed it all. Carlo still loves you."

Gillian flinched.

"And now you want our child, too."

"You can see her whenever you want," Gillian said quickly. "I won't ever take her away from you."

"It's not the same, Gillian!" She took a deep breath. "Where will you live?" Adele asked as she walked over to behind her desk and sat down.

"I'll find an apartment here…"

"You can have the one the corporation holds on Park Avenue," Adele said as she sat back.

"I don't think…"

"I don't want my daughter far from me."

"Dell, I don't know if I'll be able to afford that…" Gillian trailed off.

"Afford?" Adele seemed confused.

"I have to see."

"You are still my wife…whether you like it or not. I will not be involved in yet another scandal." Adele was beginning to lose her patience.

"But Dell…"

"Sit down!"

Gillian sat down without saying another word. The strain of the day was beginning to take a toll on her.

"I will tell you what I can live with," Adele stated leaving no room for argument.

"I am willing to listen, Dell. I want to make this work."

"I bet you do." Adele smiled sardonically. "You will live in the apartment on Park Avenue four days out of the week and the other three here." Gillian was about to speak when Adele raised her hand to stop her. "I should say my daughter, you can choose to come with her or not, that is your choice."

Gillian remained quiet so Adele continued.

"I will have money transferred to your checking account every week…"

"Dell, I don't want…"

"I am not finished." Adele seemed implacable. "You will join me on several public functions, which is not negotiable either. I have had enough ridicule to last me a lifetime," she added, fuming. "And you will sign this." Adele put a document in front of her.

Gillian looked at the document then back up at Adele again.

"What is it?"

"Adoption papers," Adele said curtly. "You aptly reminded me how I have no legal rights in this country. You know I don't need this…but there is still a part of me that is human even after knowing you." Adele growled at her.

A sob suddenly escaped Gillian. She covered her mouth with her hand as her body began to shake.

"Sign. You won't be leaving here unless it is, so sign!" Adele demanded. "If you want to be with our daughter all the time you will also have to be here with me!"

Gillian looked up as tears ran down her face. "Dell, you ask for more than I can give. I can't live here with you, Dell, I can't."

Adele straightened up and the look that she gave Gillian was the coldest any human being could receive.

"Madam, you flatter yourself. My bed will never know a cold night. I don't need you to fill it, the takers will be abundant."

"Dell…"

"You will be here and fill your role as often as needed. I will not put myself or Carlo through another scandal," Adele said with conviction.

Gillian just kept looking at her as her tears continued to fall down her face.

"This is what I can live with." Adele offered her the pen.

"Then will you let me go, Dell?" Gillian asked softly.

Adele stood up suddenly and went around the desk that separated them. She took Gillian in her arms and kissed her roughly.

Gillian found the strength she didn't know she had as she pushed her away. "No!" As soon as Dell released her, she attempted with her hand to wipe away any remnant of the kiss from Adele's mouth and was pushed away roughly.

Adele stared at her without uttering a word. Did Gillian find her lips so abhorrent that she wanted to wipe any touch between them even from her own lips?

"No. No more of this." Gillian took a step back putting more distance between her and Adele.

"What are you willing to do?" Adele asked point blank.

"Anything but this," Gillian answered quickly.

"Are you so disgusted by me?" Adele finally asked the question that had taken hold within her.

"Are you so desperate!" Gillian saw the pain the words caused visibly in Adele's face and again felt yet another wound in her own heart. She had to make Adele accept this. The best way was the most direct.

"Sign," was all Adele said as she walked back around the desk and sat down without uttering another word.

Gillian picked up the pen and signed the document without another thought.

Adele took the document and put it in the drawer on the side of the desk. She then handed Gillian an envelope.

"The keys to the apartment, a check book, and a schedule of the events I want you to attend with me for now. The dates that you will have Kateryna and the days that she will be here with me; whether you wish to be here at those times is completely up to you. It's all in this envelope."

Gillian stared at the envelope.

†

"Take it!" Adele said, raising her voice as she continued to speak. The strain was beginning to get to her. "If you break our agreement, I will take my daughter. Take the envelope, Gillian," Adele threatened.

Gillian looked up and then took the envelope. Adele could see the shaking of her hands as she took the envelope and held it against her chest.

Adele took her first real breath in what seemed like a lifetime to her. Gillian would never know what this day had cost her. Adele pushed a button on her phone, and within seconds the side door to the library opened. In walked the nanny with Catty by the hand.

"Mommy!" Catty squealed with glee as she filled Gillian's arms.

"My sweet girl," Gillian said as she kissed her daughter's hair and held her close. "I've missed you so much, baby."

"Mommy, mommy are you home?" Catty pulled away to look at her mother.

"Yes, honey, mommy is here." Gillian only said what the child needed to hear.

"Mama slept with me," Catty said proudly.

Gillian looked up towards Adele as she walked to stand towards the window again.

"Go, Miss Taylor. Catty's mother is here now. If you are needed, you will be called," Adele said coldly.

"Yes, Contessa," the woman said as she quickly exited the room.

"I brought you something, sweetie," Gillian said as she reached into her bag, pulling out a small stuffed animal shaped like a dolphin.

"Punzel!" The little girl hugged the stuffed dolphin tightly to her.

Adele smiled sadly as her eyes filled with tears. She already felt the loss of her child. Never did she imagine that she could endure the pain that she was feeling.

"I will tell cook to set another place for dinner." Adele suddenly stopped, uncertain. She turned towards Gillian. "Will you be staying with us tonight?"

Gillian nodded and Adele left them alone.

# CHAPTER FIVE

*Gillian stood leaning slightly against the rail. She loved being in this part of Washington D.C. during early spring. The cherry blossoms were in full bloom and the day was just perfect. This was her secret place. Candice had gone into the office, so Gillian had decided to see the cherry blossoms on her own. Most people who visited the capital never realized that there was this wonderful time. A special time during spring that lasted for perhaps only a few days. Rows of cherry blossoms along the Potomac River that created the most beautiful effect she had ever seen. As you walked along the river you were enveloped in a sea of pink that seemed to soothe the senses and fill you with a sense of beauty and peace rarely felt or seen. The perfume of a warm and beautiful day accompanied by the sound of the river was sheer contentment. Since she had moved to Washington D.C. with Candice three years before, she had never missed it. Today was perfect. She walked along the Jefferson Memorial, her favorite of all the places in the famous city. She walked around it and just leaned against the rail, listening as the river slowly went merrily on its way. She closed her eyes and took in the sweetness of the sunny day. Her face turned up and she smiled.*

*"You are truly beautiful, cara mia," a velvety voice said next to her ear.*

*Gillian turned slowly, somehow not surprised that Adele would be there. Adele leaned forward and she did not back away. Their lips touched briefly before Adele took a step back and chose to stand next to her.*

*"Adele…"*

*"No, give me just a little time, it is all I ask," Adele murmured and looked towards the water sadly. "I hurt, cara. I have never hurt like this before. You are so deep in here." Adele pointed to the middle of her chest.*

*Gillian looked at her, neither angry nor surprised. Those words from anyone else might have sounded theatrical but they rang true from the woman standing next to her. Somehow this was very much Adele's way. She was by far the most interesting, complex woman Gillian had ever met.*

*"Adele…"*

*"Just a little part of today…"*

*Gillian turned and both stood quietly staring at one another.*

*"You love this place," Adele stated.*

*"Yes," Gillian answered, smiling shyly.*

*"It is so you, the beauty of this secret place." Adele looked around noticing the few people near them. "Not many visit this place I see and yet...I do see what calls to you, cara," Adele said as she turned to face her. "It is all you."*

*Gillian wanted, as always, to just surrender to the dark-haired Contessa that had begun to haunt her dreams, but she couldn't. She had given her word to Candice and that she could not break. Adele was a desire that she had to suppress.*

*"I am not asking for anything, just a little time with you," Adele said sadly. "I know that I have not touched your heart. It is almost just that it is this way." Adele looked away. "You have cut deeply into me, and I cannot pull you out."*

*"Adele, I can't..."*

*"I know, you are in love with someone else."*

*Gillian opened her mouth to only close it again.*

*"I will be leaving for Firenze tomorrow. I just wanted to see you one more time."*

*Gillian looked towards her now.*

*"I want a few hours. Can you give me that?" Adele's head leaned down. When she heard no answer, she looked towards Gillian and faced her. "Just a few hours, cara,*

*that's all I ask. On my honor, I will leave you and walk away."*

*Gillian said nothing and only nodded as Adele smiled. "Walk with me."*

*They walked side by side slowly and quietly down the path surrounded by the pink hew of the blossoms, and occasionally would take turns shyly smiling one at the other.*

†

*Along their walk they sat down on a bench. Adele closed her eyes and tried to take it all in. She wanted to take this perfect picture of Gillian with her.*

*"When will you be back?" Gillian broke the silence.*

*"I will not be back," Adele answered as she opened her eyes, avoiding looking at Gillian.*

*"Why?"*

*"Because you will be here."*

*"Adele…"*

*Adele faced her now. "I love you. I have never been in love before, and I know that I have done this all wrong. I don't know how to act or what to say since all that I have said has been wrong! Nothing that I have done has been right." Adele stood up and took a few steps away from her. With her back to Gillian now she continued to speak. "I have always gotten what I wanted. I have never needed. Now that I find myself needing, I…"*

*Adele took a few more steps away. "I tried to stay away from you, and all I could think of while away was when I would be coming back here to see you again. You are all I think about. In the beginning, I don't know what it was...finding all the things that you liked, where you lived, who you knew, what you did. And then one day I realized that you were in every thought, every breath...I wanted to include you or the thought of you in every aspect of my life. I wanted...I didn't only want you for an affair like I have always taken people, Gillian. I wanted you in my life, for the rest of my life."*

†

*Gillian was speechless. She could neither speak nor move. The words had touched her heart as no words had ever touched her before, but surely, this was all insane. Love didn't happen this way, did it?*

*"You hardly know me," Gillian said in disbelief.*

*Adele faced her in desperation. "I have always known you!"*

*"You just want to get me to bed, Adele." Gillian fought her desire to just give in. She had given herself reasons against feeling what she knew had been growing inside her.*

*"Yes, I want you, Gillian. I want you like I have never wanted in my whole life." Adele did not deny it. "Why, is it wrong to want you?"*

*Gillian turned away.*

*"I want all of you. I want to walk with you and share your day. I want to make love to you during the night and wake up with you in my arms. I want all the things that I have denied every other lover. I want to wake up with you," Adele said with conviction.*

*Gillian remained quiet.*

*Adele took a deep breath. "Goodbye, Gillian. Thank you for giving me this time with you. I won't interfere in your life anymore. I sincerely hope that you are happy."*

*When Adele didn't hear her speak, she started to walk away.*

*"Wait," Gillian said weakly and stood on legs that could barely sustain her.*

*Adele turned around and saw the fear and indecision in her eyes. She quickly closed the distance between them and took her in her arms. "Love me, cara. I promise you that I will make you glad you do." Adele's lips sealed the unspoken promise.*

*Gillian's eyes filled with tears, and she pulled away slowly as she looked into Adele's eyes. "I promised her I would never hurt her."*

*"I won't let you go." Adele kissed her passionately once more as she pulled her back into her embrace.*

*"Adele...Adele."* Gillian *cried as she clung to the woman that was tightly holding her. "I have tried so hard not to love you. I have tried so hard..."*

*"Cara...ti amo, cara mia..."* Adele *kissed her then pulled her again into a fierce embrace. "You are mine, cara...you are mine. Forever mine..."*

✝

Candice *walked into the house and instantly knew that there was something wrong.* Gillian *walked into the living room not quite looking at her.*

*"Hello, babe."* Candice *walked up to her to kiss her, and* Gillian *turned her face away.* Candice *was about to ask what was wrong when she noticed Adele entering the room.*

*"What is she doing here?"* Candice *demanded.*

*"Candice..."* Gillian *said softly but could not continue.*

Candice *turned towards her and saw the strain visible in her lover's face. "What did she do? Did she hurt you?"*

*"No..."* Gillian *could barely speak. "I'm sorry, Candy...I'm so sorry."*

Candice *turned her anger towards the woman that had suddenly become her worst nightmare. "You bitch!"*

*"Candice, don't,"* Gillian *pleaded.*

*"Did you fuck her? How could you?" Candice accused Gillian.*

*"Don't speak to her that way!" Adele immediately took a step forward.*

*"You shut the fuck up!" Candice was heading for Adele when Gillian stepped in front of her.*

*"Candice, it's not her."*

*Candice looked from Gillian to Adele and back to Gillian again in confusion.*

*"I didn't want to fall in love with her but I did," Gillian said miserably.*

*"She's no good, Gillian. She's no good."*

*"Candice, I love her," Gillian said softly. "I loved her from the first instant. I didn't want to, but I do."*

*Candice stared at Adele murderously. "Well, you got your way, didn't you. Did you fuck her in our bed?"*

*"If you don't shut your filthy mouth, I will shut it for you, cagna!" Adele grew angrier and angrier.*

*"You disgust me, get out of my house!" Candice took a few steps away from Gillian.*

*"I'm sorry, Candy. I'm sorry…"*

*"Get out!"*

*"I…"*

*"Get out!" Candice yelled as she turned to face Gillian once more. "Get out of my sight. She's a user, Gillian. How long do you think she is going to want you? She*

*will eventually get tired of fucking you and just discard you like she discards everything else in her life."*

*Candice walked towards a drawer in a nearby desk and pulled out a file. "Here, read this. Read all about your precious Contessa. Read about how honourable she truly is. You won't last a week in her world."*

*Candice shoved the file into Gillian's hands and walked away from her.*

*Adele walked up behind Gillian and pulled her to her; she then took the file from Gillian's hands and threw it to the floor. "Still, she is in love with me. And I am taking her with me," Adele hissed.*

*"Adele..." Gillian pulled away.*

*"Get out, please," Candice begged.*

*"My pleasure, andiamo cara." Adele growled and took Gillian by the hand.*

*"Adele, I need to talk to her."*

*"No!"*

*"She's right, Gillian. We have nothing to talk about. Just go," Candice replied miserably.*

*"Please, Adele, wait for me outside," Gillian pleaded.*

*"Cara, no..."*

*"Please."*

*Adele looked deeply into Gillian's eyes then nodded and headed for the door. She stopped suddenly and turned towards Candice. "I have not fucked her as you put it, and it is not because I didn't want to but rather that she could not betray her promise to you. I love her." She turned and left.*

*Gillian turned towards Candice who was staring at her.*

*"You lied to me."*

*"Candice, I never meant to lie...I can't explain what happened. She is just something I can't fight. I never wanted to hurt you," Gillian said gently.*

*"I trusted you. Please just tell me you didn't sleep with her on our bed. Please just tell me that." Candice cried miserably as eyes pleaded.*

*"No, we didn't. I wouldn't do that to you. I haven't slept with her, Candy. I haven't. What she said is true. I couldn't betray you that way."*

*Candice stared at her in disbelief then the truth of the words hit her. "What?"*

*"I haven't...we haven't. I..."*

*Candice stared at Gillian and saw the battle that was raging in her still. "Gillian, are you sure about this?" Candice asked gently.*

*"I can't fight her. What I feel is so strong that I can't fight it anymore." Tears spilled from her eyes and slid down her cheeks. "I..."*

*"She is not good enough for you, she will never do what you need. How could you choose her instead of me?" Candice wept softly.*

*Candice wanted so badly to hate her, but somehow loving Gillian was something that had always been inside her. She had loved Gillian her whole life and she knew that it would always be this way. They had grown up together. Candice knew that Gillian had not lied to her. She also knew that she could still have a part of Gillian if she was careful now. Candice took a few steps closer, and Gillian looked up.*

*"Candy..."*

*"I know." Candice took her into her arms. "If you ever need me, I will be here."*

*"Candy." Gillian cried all the harder*

*Candice stood by the window and watched as Gillian walked up to Adele. Adele took her into her arms and her eyes at that moment met Candice's. Adele had won for now.*

†

*"Amore, amore mio," Adele whispered into Gillian's ear as she held her fiercely.*

*She had never been more afraid in her whole life as she patiently waited for Gillian to come out. It took all the strength she possessed not to go back inside and physically bring her out. A part of her kept screaming* go get her! *and the other kept repeating that Gillian had to do this her own way or she would never truly be happy. The few minutes that she waited seemed to last a lifetime. When she finally saw Gillian walk out the front door, Adele had never in her life felt such relief. She took a deep breath, slowly and gently, never for one moment releasing Gillian from her embrace as she walked her into the waiting car.*

†

*Candice watched Adele guide Gillian into the black limousine. She thought her heart would break as she tried to breathe. The last thing she remembered seeing was Adele looking in her direction once more and raising her chin defiantly. Candice's hands clenched into fists; she hated Adele Visconti. She didn't blame Gillian; a part of her had already forgiven her, but Adele Visconti was another matter altogether.*

*"She is not good enough for you, Gilly, she is not good enough for you…" Candice wept openly as she saw the limousine drive away.*

†

*Adele held Gillian tightly to her as she wept. She would show her the world. Gillian would know all the beauty that existed, and she would be the one to give it to her. Adele's heart overflowed with happiness. Never had she felt such rapture nor such triumph. She now held in her arms her heart's desire. This was a new life; she would deal with all*

70

*that would follow. Having Gillian was worth any cost, and she was willing to pay it.*

†

*Dinner had been by candlelight and somehow the most romantic music Gillian had ever heard seemed to come from nowhere and fill the dining hall. They had both dressed for dinner. Adele had not left her side since they had arrived earlier. The house was beautiful in every way. She was speechless when she entered as her eyes went from lush Persian carpets to the works of art that hung on the walls. It was all so surreal, in some ways like she was in a fairytale, but it was all true. Then Adele had taken her hand and walked her down to the dining room for dinner. The champagne, the lobster, the luscious dessert had all blended into the perfection of their first evening together.*

*Adele was a master of romance. She had once boasted that every woman could be had and yet not one of her conquests had ever possessed her heart. Gillian had surprised her in so many ways. Gillian, she had waited for, cajoled, romanced, and Gillian, unlike any other, she loved. She held Gillian's hand as she slowly led her up the staircase to their bedroom. She thought her heart would burst out of her chest with its pounding. She had never felt such want for a woman; it was more, so much more than just love. For the first time in her life the Contessa trembled with anticipation.*

*No other woman had taken her as Gillian had without so much as a mere touch.*

*When they finally reached the bedroom door Adele reached for the doorknob and stopped as Gillian covered her hand. Her eyes moved up and all the doubt that Gillian might have had disappeared as soon as she looked into her Contessa's eyes. Because what Gillian saw was love.*

*"I'm afraid," Gillian said softly.*

*Adele's hand went up to her face and caressed it. "I am filled with such love for you, amore mio. It is love, I swear it." Adele wanted, needed Gillian to understand that this was something new for her. Adele waited for a sign. Gillian had to want her as much as she wanted Gillian. For the first time in her life, Adele was nervous.*

*Gillian swayed towards her, and her forehead leaned against Adele's lips.*

*"Come, vieni con me amore mio," Adele said as she opened the door and walked inside.*

*The room was covered only by the light of the moon shining through the big French doors that led onto a balcony. Gillian took a few steps in front of Adele then turned around and faced her.*

*Adele walked up to her, and her eyes began caressing Gillian's face and then travelled down her body. When her eyes came back up to meet the one's of the woman in front of her, they were filled with passion and love, so much love that it made her heart ache.*

*"You are so beautiful, tesoro." Adele's velvety voice was like a caress to Gillian's senses.*

*Adele took a step closer towards her without touching her. She willed Gillian's body to sway forward. Then, still without her hands touching her, she leaned forward, and her lips slowly and seductively travelled from Gillian's ear lobe to the edge of her mouth. "I'm going to make you mine. And I will love you till the end of my life, amore mio. This I swear."*

*Gillian's head fell back as Adele's mouth travelled down her neck and then Adele's arms pulled their bodies closer still. Adele's hands travelled up, caressing her and slid both straps of her dress down Gillian's shoulders. At that moment both women looked into each other's eyes without moving. Gillian took a step back without breaking eye contact and continued to slide the straps down, baring her breasts before Adele.*

*Adele's eyes turned molten and every fibre in her being began to throb inside her. "Gillian…" she managed to say, barely breathing.*

*Gillian held her hand out and Adele took it.*

*Adele stood before her and suddenly her eyes filled with tears. Gillian brushed them lovingly away.*

*"I love you, Gillian," Adele said softly as she kissed her lovingly. The tenderness of the kiss began to gradually demand more, and Gillian's mouth opened and allowed Adele to begin her possession.*

Slowly Adele lowered her onto the bed and between kisses and caresses they both lay half clothed. Caresses that began slowly became demanding and possession of one another became a paramount need.

"Cara..." Adele pinned Gillian beneath her, and their bodies fused in a primal effort to become one.

"Ah..." Gillian let her head fall back as she felt Adele's caresses moving lower. The throbbing between her legs begged for release and when she felt Adele's touch, her world began to spin as she felt Adele's mouth take possession of her. "Dell, oh God, Dell..."

Their love making had begun slowly, with tenderness, touching, exploring, feeling, kissing, and tasting each other's skin until the fire and passion that had bound them from the very first moment erupted and their bodies fused, melting into one another with screams of pleasure that filled their worlds.

During the night the light coming from the large window awakened Adele and the warmth of the woman in her arms filled her with more happiness than she thought possible. Adele tightened her arms to hold her closer still.

†

"I love you, Dell," Gillian said softly.

*Gillian turned around to face her and gently caressed the face of her dark-haired Contessa. Adele held her hand, turning it to kiss the inside of it.*

*"I need you like the air I breathe, Gillian," Adele said passionately. And at that moment Gillian heard the fragility of that statement.*

*Gillian smiled softly and leaned to kiss her. She then pressed the Contessa down onto the bed and began to make love to her with all the tenderness she felt inside for her. She sensed that Adele needed this, this tenderness from her. It was at this moment that Gillian took her own possession and they both truly became one.*

†

*Adele had never had anyone love her as Gillian had done. She had never allowed anyone to get that close. The gentleness of her lover's touch had gone beyond anything she had ever experienced. Adele wept from the beauty of the union. Gillian held her tighter and told her over and over again that she would never leave. And thus, began their life together, based on a promise of love and a forever.*

†

Dinner was a formal affair. Gillian concentrated on the baby that was first excited at being at the table on her highchair during dinner with both her mothers. Adele barely spoke unless Catty addressed her.

Towards the end of the dinner, Catty began to look visibly sleepy and cranky.

"Time for beddy-bye, sweet pea," Gillian said gently as she began to take her daughter out of the highchair.

"No… no, Mommy, no." Catty began to fuss.

"Let me." Adele came to her aid and Gillian stepped aside. "Does my *principesa* want to fly?" she asked indulgently.

The child immediately smiled and nodded. "Come along then, Mama will fly you upstairs."

Catty held her arms out for her mother to take her and giggled. Her little fingers beckoned to be picked up.

Gillian noticed how the maid, clearing the table, smiled secretly at seeing that the austere Contessa was so very human after all. No one doubted that she adored her child. And Gillian felt the pain inside her magnify once more. She then took a step back and repeated to herself again, *I am doing the right thing, it is better this way.*

"Come along, *cara*, let's put this little one to bed." In her joy of her daughter, Adele had forgotten their estrangement and had called Gillian her beloved. Adele continued making buzzing noises and never realized what she had said. The child began to giggle and wiggle and continued encouraging her mother to make the airplane sounds.

Gillian followed them up the stairs. They both helped get the little girl to bed; both helping her put on her pajamas and both stood by her bedside after kissing her good night.

"Good night, baby," Gillian said as she pulled up the covers over her daughter.

"Night, Mommy," Catty said as she gave her mother another hug.

Adele then leaned down and kissed her daughter goodnight.

"Mama, sleep with me?" the sleepy child asked Adele.

"No, my darling, not tonight," Adele said as she caressed the child's hair, leaning down, and kissing her on the forehead once more.

"Mommy can sleep with us too, Mama," the little girl insisted.

"Not tonight, little one, not tonight," Adele replied tenderly.

"Okay, you sleep with Mommy," Catty finally conceded, turning on her side, grabbing her stuffed toy, and falling quickly asleep.

Both women walked out of the room quietly, closing the door behind them. Once in the hallway Adele faced Gillian. "You can use the bedroom to the other side of Catty's room. It has been prepared for you. I know that you want to be close to her."

"All right, thank you, Adele." Gillian felt weak suddenly and swayed unexpectedly, and without warning, towards Adele.

She was immediately held in a warm embrace. An embrace that she craved to surrender to but knew she must not. Gillian pulled herself away.

"Gillian…?"

"I'm so sorry. I think I'm just tired," Gillian apologized and walked away towards her bedroom.

†

Adele stood without moving, looking at her as she walked away wondering how she would ever survive losing the woman that, to her shame, she still loved. She felt ashamed of wanting someone that had betrayed her, was sleeping with someone else and obviously no longer wanted her. She had always been the one that did the chasing, the one that others wanted and now she felt the feeling of being rejected. Rejection had never been a part of her vocabulary. She had felt rejection from her mother once too many times. Adele learned early on not to need, to just take and never allow anyone close enough to hurt her. Gillian had been someone that she did not want to hide from and now she was paying for that folly she told herself. Her eyes stayed on Gillian until she entered the other bedroom. Adele could not stop her mind from asking herself so many questions; like how can I never kiss her again, how can I never hold her again, how can I breathe without her again? She found that the pressure she constantly felt in the middle of her chest was allowing her to hardly draw a breath of late.

†

Gillian walked into the room that she had decorated only two years before. This had been her home, and now she was just a visitor. She ran her fingers over the comforter that had taken her a month to choose and smiled at the memory. Then she sat down and took in a deep breath. Her new journey had begun, and she would see it through. Gillian reached over to the telephone on the nightstand and proceeded to call Candice.

"You are what?" Candice could not believe what she had just heard. "Are you crazy?"

"This is what it will take to make things work," Gillian said rubbing her temple. Her headache was unbearable.

"Gillian, I don't think this is a good idea. I'm afraid for you. She won't be the same now, Gilly. Her true colours will come out." Candice wanted her words to strike Gillian and they did.

"I... I have to believe that she will keep her word, Candice. I can't fight her... and I don't want to." The exhaustion could be felt over the telephone.

Candice remained quiet. She could hear the weariness in Gillian's voice. "She..."

"I'm tired, Candice."

"I know you are, baby, I know you are. I'm sorry that it's so hard. You have a headache, don't you?" Candice asked sympathetically.

"Yes…" Gillian said as she began to weep. "How did you know?"

"You always get a headache when you are stressed, sweetheart," Candice said tenderly.

Gillian then began to sob. "Oh Candy, why? Why would this happen? Oh God, why?" Gillian held on to the phone and wept inconsolably.

"Oh Gilly, please don't cry, baby. Please don't cry. God! I wish I was there!" Candice took a deep breath. "Gilly, baby, please, please."

"I'm sorry…"

"There is nothing to be sorry about. I know how hard this is. I will stand by you no matter what, babe. You are not alone, okay? Remember that. Will you remember that?" Candice waited for the answer patiently.

"Yes, yes I will," Gillian finally said a little calmer. "Goodnight Candice…"

Before she finished saying goodnight, she heard the door open, and instantly she knew that Adele had heard her say goodnight to Candice.

Gillian hung up the phone and stood up to face her. Adele stared at her with such hatred that it physically hurt her to see it.

After a moment Adele spoke. "I thought you might need these." She handed Gillian a negligee and a few other toiletries.

"Yes, thank you." Gillian looked down at the clothing and then looked back up into Adele's eyes. "Thank you."

Adele took a step forward and brushed a tear away. "She doesn't like the arrangement, does she?" As tender as the touch had been her words sounded as cold as steel.

Gillian merely kept looking into her eyes.

"She will have you back soon enough. Don't embarrass me, Gillian. Another scandal I will not allow. Keep your lover away from the public eye or I will take Catty away and you will never see her again," Adele hissed at her.

Gillian's eyes overflowed with tears. "Dell, why are you being so cruel?"

Adele said nothing, the coldness in her eyes unyielding. "I don't owe you anything," she finally said, seething.

Gillian reached out to touch her and found her hand held in a tight grip.

"Don't you ever touch me!" Adele spoke through her teeth barely controlling the anger within as she suddenly pulled her roughly to her. "Missing my touch already, *cara*?"

Her voice held the menace she was barely keeping below the surface.

"Dell, please." Gillian let her forehead lean forward until it touched the side of Adele's temple. "Don't hate me, please," Gillian pleaded miserably.

Adele could feel Gillian's breath on her skin and closed her eyes. She released her hold and Gillian's arms came up around her neck as she wept.

"Please Dell…I…" A sob racketed Gillian's body as her arms tightened around Adele's neck.

Gillian clung to her, and this brought to the surface too many emotions for Adele to process. Holding Gillian like this another minute would surely kill her. Her body did not register that the woman in her arms was no longer her lover and the need to touch her, love her, came alive faster than she could control it. Adele's arms came up to hold her. But just as suddenly, the pain of the betrayal was all that she could feel. She could not be Gillian's friend. What Gillian was asking for was impossible. She could no more be her friend than she would be her lover ever again. Adele removed Gillian's arms from around her neck and walked out of her arms and out of the room without saying a word.

†

Gillian fell on her knees as soon as she saw the door close. She knew that in her moment of weakness she had placed another scar on Adele's heart.

# CHAPTER SIX

"Hello…"

"Contessa, we have a cab here at the gate. The driver says it is picking up Mrs. Visconti. Should I let him through?" The guard waited for an answer nervously. There was obviously trouble in paradise, and he didn't want to be in the middle of it in any way. The Contessa valued her privacy, and he did not want to know more than he should.

"Pay him for coming out here and send him away. It was an error." Saying no more, the line went dead.

The security guard then spoke to the cab driver. "Sorry for the inconvenience, buddy. No cab needed. Here is twenty dollars for your trouble."

"All right, Mack. Thanks."

The cab backed out and away from the gate. The guard looked towards the house and noticed a few lights coming on. He shook his head as he mumbled, "Marital bliss, you gotta love it."

†

Gillian stood by one of the windows that looked over the front lawn of the estate. Her cab should be arriving any moment now. It had been a mistake to stay here overnight. Her head was throbbing, and her chest ached. Everything inside her was filling with a pain she could not bear. She wanted to cry but she had no more tears left. Being away at this moment—no, running away—was the only thing that would give her any hope of surviving this. Dell was too formidable of an opponent. Dell had always been stronger, more persistent, and Gillian knew that if she didn't put some real distance between them things were only going to get worse. Candice had been right. It had been madness, sheer madness for her to have stayed.

"Where did you think you were going?" a voice in the dark room said softly. Its softness however could not hide the coldness.

Gillian turned around trying to find Adele in the darkness that covered the room.

"Running away so soon? Couldn't you stay away from her for one night?" The words seemed to get harsher and the timbre of them more menacing. "I can take care of your need *cara*... I always have before."

Suddenly Adele was right in front of her pulling roughly towards her. Adele's whole body was pressed against her. She felt Adele's breath on her cheek. Gillian tried to take in a breath and found it impossible. Adele's lips were running lightly on her cheek. "I want you." The words were unmistakably raw and sensual. Adele's body was beckoning, and her hands were pulling her closer while caressing her.

The warmth fused them both, sparking between them. All that could be heard was the strained breathing coming from them both. Strained and bursting, rushing to a release that only the body pressed against it could provide.

Gillian pressed forward and her eyes closed as she lost herself in the recognition of the passion that had always existed between them. "Dell..."

Adele's hands travelled down and as her palms cupped Gillian's ass, she squeezed, and pulled her closer to her as her mouth took control of Gillian's lips.

Gillian's mouth opened and a moan escaped her. "Oh Dell,..." she moaned as her hand went up to Adele's neck. Her hands travelled up to feel the fullness of the dark mane that she had loved and as she did, she felt Adele's arms pulling her closer still. The fire that had always consumed them when they were this close to one another became a raging volcano running out of control.

†

Adele's mouth kissed her with such raw passion and desperation that all the anger she had felt while looking for Gillian through the dark had simply vanished. All that she felt was the need to hold onto her life. Because that is what Gillian was to her. Gillian was life, love, passion, and all the other baser emotions that had once been held in check but were now running rampant within her, and she could no more control her desire than she could her love for her.

Adele's mouth travelled down her neck and her hands began to quickly pull up Gillian's dress. She had to touch her; she had to feel Gillian's wetness so that she could once more know that it had been she who had made her feel. Her ardour made her rush; she pulled aside Gillian's panties, and her fingers found the folds that indeed were hot and wet.

"I want you, oh God, I want you," she whispered in Gillian's ear. "I want to be inside you… I need to be inside you." Adele's voice was horse in desperation.

†

Gillian's eyes suddenly opened wide and roughly pushed her away. The look of pain in Adele's eyes were almost her undoing. She had never seen a look of such betrayal mirrored at her. Adele just stood in front of her looking like someone had just torn her heart out of her chest; and of course, someone had. Gillian wrapped her arms around herself and began to weep. "I can't... I can't."

✝

Adele suddenly felt the rage rise within her and the growl that came out of her not only frightened Gillian but made her take a few steps away. Adele wrapped her arms around herself protectively without thinking.

Instead of running away, Gillian went to her. "I'm sorry..." she said as her hand reached out for Adele.

Adele grabbed her hand and just stood staring at her. Her grip had become solid rock. Gillian was not going anywhere.

"I'm going to fuck you," Adele said between her teeth. Her eyes had taken on a glazed look of madness that Gillian had never seen before. "I'm going to fuck you until I get you out of my soul." As she finished speaking, she yanked Gillian hard against her.

"You promised me that you wouldn't hurt me..." Gillian said gently. "I know that I've hurt you. You said you would always love me and never hurt me Dell, remember?" Tears ran down her face freely as she said this.

"I'm going to fuck you," Adele said as her grip tightened. "You are mine," she whispered as her mouth caressed Gillian's ear as one hand began to touch her while the other kept a hold of her.

Gillian tried pushing her away. "No, not anymore," Gillian said softly as her eyes filled with tears. "You have to let me go, Dell, please."

Adele's hands were holding her in place again. Her hold was so hard that Gillian winced from the pain of it trying to pull away.

"I married you. I paid for the privilege." Adele growled. Adele then pulled her closer roughly and her eyes looked directly into Gillian's. "I will give you the freedom you want. But I will take what is mine when I want it."

Gillian's eyes filled with fear and then with sadness. "And then what will you do?" she asked sadly.

Adele's eyes suddenly wavered and she could see the uncertainty that the question had produced. Adele suddenly felt the darkness looming, waiting to take her. The darkness that had been an old friend; the bottomless pit. All this she knew too well and that is what she would have if she took this from Gillian. What would become of them? All these things were going through her mind as she released Gillian and took a step back.

"You are still my wife..." Adele whispered. She could not find the way to just let go. She bowed her head and turned away from Gillian. "Go back to bed, I will not bother you. Catty will be disappointed if you are not here in the morning." The defeat was apparent in her voice.

Gillian began to walk past her then stopped. "Dell?"

"Good night, Gillian," she said softly. "No more words tonight. You have what you wanted." Adele walked away from her leaving her standing in the darkness.

"Dell…" Gillian whispered into the emptiness of the room wanting something she could no longer have.

†

In the morning they all had breakfast together and the mood was somber. They ate quietly and the only noise heard was that made of the cutlery and the cups being picked up and put down, and of course complaints made by Catty who didn't want to eat her breakfast.

"Come on baby, eat for Mommy," Gillian cooed. "Just a little more, please."

Catty would turn her head away and shake it. "No."

Adele would look now and then from her newspaper while she drank her coffee.

"She is being stubborn. She will not eat for you." Adele went back to her coffee and newspaper.

"You think you can do better?" Gillian tried hard to suppress the anger that could be heard in her voice.

Adele looked up sharply. "I am not criticizing your method. Our daughter is stubborn."

Gillian stared at her for a moment and then looked down. "I'm sorry." Gillian looked up as Adele stared at her a bit longer then went back to her newspaper.

Gillian went back to feeding her daughter. After a moment or two she had worked up the courage to speak to Adele again.

"Dell, I am going to the apartment after breakfast, and I want to take Catty with me." Gillian raised her eyes to meet the one's now staring at her.

Adele said nothing for a moment then went back to reading her newspaper. After a moment she spoke but did not look up. "You can take whatever you like to make Catty as comfortable as possible. I want you both ..." She stopped abruptly then continued, "I want her back by the week's end."

Adele got up quickly and walked over to her daughter. She leaned down and gently kissed her on the head. "Be good for Mommy, my *principessa,*" she said softly.

Catty looked up and smiled at her mother who sadly smiled back at her. "I will miss you little one, but I will see you soon."

Adele then quickly proceeded to leave the room. She stopped at the door with her back still turned to them. "I will speak to Marco. He can make all the necessary arrangements and help you with whatever you need."

As Gillian was about to thank her Adele was already gone. Gillian turned back to look at her little girl and saw her daughter's lower lip quivering. "Mama?"

"It's only going to be for a few days, baby, then we will see Mama again. You and I are going to have lots of fun." Gillian smiled as she felt her eyes filling quickly with tears too.

Gillian hugged her little girl. It was going to be for only a little while. She needed to feel her child close to her. Adele would have her back soon enough. Gillian knew that Adele would always love Catty and that thought made the ache inside her all the more bearable. Her little girl would be okay. Catty would always be taken care of and loved.

†

Adele looked through the glass as they got into a cab and left. Gillian had insisted on the cab instead of the limousine, and she had given in at the end. What Gillian did not know is that she was not to take another step in her life that Adele would not know about. Her hand touched the coldness of the windowpane. She could swear that the cold ran all the way into her heart. Tears did not come. How could they, she had no more tears to shed. Her head leaned into the coolness of the windowpane and her hand began to hit the glass until the glass gave way and she stood on pieces of broken glass as blood fell on the shattered pieces that lay on the floor.

The library door opened, and Marco walked in and quickly lifted her hand and put pressure on the cut to make it stop bleeding.

"Contessa, we have to get you to a hospital," he insisted.

She turned to him, surprised to see him suddenly. "Why?"

He noticed the glassiness of her gaze. "The wound, Contessa. It must be taken care of and closed properly. I will call for the car. Please put pressure here while I make the phone call."

She did as he said without response. She stared at the blood, unable to recall how it had happened.

Marco went to the nearest phone on a nearby table but kept a close eye on the Contessa. Something was wrong; something was very wrong.

"Some wounds never heal and never close," Adele whispered to herself.

"What, Contessa?" He strained to hear what she was saying while he was making his call.

"Nothing, nothing…" Adele looked down at her hand and saw the blood running through her fingers. Her blood, the liquid that made life possible. How wrong people were. She was already dead inside.

## CHAPTER SEVEN

---

Gillian had called Candice and asked her to meet her in front of the apartment building.

Candice ran up to them and hugged them as soon as she saw them. She held on as they both cried. "I'm so happy to see you. God, I'm so happy to see you," Candice said as she kissed Catty, then kissed Gillian lightly on the lips. "Are you okay?"

"Yes," Gillian said and smiled a little.

"Why are we meeting here?"

"Here is where we will be living."

"What?" Candice looked from Gillian to the building back to Gillian again.

"It's a long story. Catty needs a nap, come up with me."

Candice was about to say something, then just closed her mouth and followed Gillian into the building.

When they walked inside the wealth was evident in the furnishings and the décor of the lobby with its raw iron designs and mahogany accents. Wealth oozed from the uniform of the man that met them in the lobby to the oriental carpets on the floor. Candice looked around ,trying hard not to be impressed. Gillian went straight for the elevator but was stopped before entering by a very elegantly dressed gentleman who knew her by name and was clearly ecstatic to be welcoming her.

"Mrs. Visconti, if there is anything that you need, please call down and ask for me. My name is Edward, and I am the manager of The Rosemont. The Contessa called earlier and requested that I personally see to your needs while you are here. Please don't hesitate to let me know what you need, Mrs. Visconti."

"Thank you, I will."

"Some groceries were delivered to take care of anything immediate that you might need. The chef is, of course, at your disposal. All you have to do is call down and your request will be brought up to you."

"Thank you, Edward," Gillian said as she entered the elevator.

Candice followed quietly in awe. She knew that Adele was wealthy, but this was suddenly overwhelming. Immediately she understood that if Adele truly wanted to fight them in the courts she would win if for no other reason than the money that she could afford to spend. She would be able to tie them up in legal work for years at the very least.

"Good afternoon then, Mrs. Visconti."

"Good afternoon, Edward," Gillian answered as the doors closed.

Candice stared at Gillian in silence. Catty was sucking her thumb and seemed sleepy. Candice looked down at the floor trying to understand what was happening. Whatever she would say to Gillian about this new development would have to wait till Catty was taken care of.

The elevator door opened to yet another door. Gillian removed a key from her pocket, turned the handle and proceeded to walk through. Candice again followed without saying a word.

The door opened into an ample living room. All of New York City seemed at their feet as they walked in and were met by a wall of glass. The furniture was evidently expensive, and the antiques and Persian carpets were of immaculate quality. Candice looked around in shock and fear. What the hell was going on?

"I'm going to put Catty down for a nap and then we can talk, okay?" Gillian said before she walked out of the room. Candice walked around the room lightly touching the obvious pieces of art that decorated the area.

Candice finally sat down and stared quietly at the expansive metropolis visible through the glass wall before her. Nothing had prepared her for anything of what was happening. If this had been done intentionally by Adele, she had proved her point. Perhaps, there was no point, she thought suddenly as she leaned forward and ran her tired fingers through her hair. She was clearly out of her element. She would never be able to compete with this. And then suddenly her eyes filled with tears as she remembered she wouldn't have to. Gillian was with her now by her own choice, and that was all that mattered. This was her chance to fill the void once left by Gillian. Candice would treasure every minute and every joy. All that she knew was that she had Gillian now and their future for as long as it lasted.

†

The blooms were coming in early this year. Everything seemed alive. The colors were shyly coming forth and the abundance of scents were beginning to make its comeback from the dead imposed by winter. Adele stood quietly, leaning against a veranda, waiting for the sun to disappear into the horizon. Soon the world would be in darkness. Soon the night would come again, and thoughts of Gillian in Candice's arms would torment her until the sun once again covered the earth. Her eyes shut as a fierce pain went through her that she thought would kill her very soul.

"Hello, darling." A deeply sensual woman's voice made Adele turn around.

"Margot, I wasn't expecting you," Adele said as her semblance changed completely, taking on a polite and aloof manner. She walked over to the woman and kissed her on both cheeks.

"I have been trying to reach you for the past few days. I stopped by the house and Marco said you were here. I was surprised since you are never in New York at this time of year." She smiled as she started to sit on a nearby bench. Margot looked at the blooms around them and smiled as she focused on Adele again.

"I have been here for the last few days. Is there something in particular that you wanted?" Adele asked politely, sitting on the bench as well.

Margot looked up and searched the dark eyes looking at her. "Is there something wrong?"

"Nothing, why?" Adele looked away at the sun that was quickly disappearing. "Soon it will be dusk," she said sadly.

Margot looked from Adele to the horizon and back to Adele again. "You know, when Mother married your father, I don't think I was prepared for it."

Adele turned and gave Margot her full attention and a surprised expression appeared in Adele's face.

"And when you and Matteo were born, I wasn't exactly happy." Margot smiled a little and looked down to her hands. "Until I saw you. You were the most beautiful child." Margot looked up and stared into her sister's eyes. "I think I fell in love with you right then."

Adele looked at her with surprise.

"I was sent away to boarding school soon after. You and Matteo at least came home for the holidays at the same time. What I am trying to say, Adele, is that we didn't exactly grow up together, you and I, but I do love you. And I can tell when something is wrong."

Adele looked away, needing so desperately to speak to someone and yet not quite sure that Margot should be the one she should confide in.

"When Matteo died, I thought that you and I might grow closer together. After all, you and I are all we will have when Mama is gone. Then came Gillian... Gillian, where is Gillian?"

Adele did not turn to look at her nor did she speak.

"Oh, I see," Margot said sadly.

"There is nothing to see. Gillian is visiting her parents with Catty." Adele rose suddenly. "Is that why you came?"

"Adele, I am not..."

"Tell Mama that Gillian and I are still very happy. Nothing is wrong." Adele started walking away until Margot grabbed her arm and stopped her.

"Adele, Matteo is gone but I am here," Margot pleaded.

"All is well, Margot." Adele began to walk away, then suddenly turned towards her sister. "Forgive me my manners. Will you be staying the night?"

"Yes, thank you."

"Very well, I shall have a room prepared for you and let cook know that you will be staying for dinner."

"Thank you," Margot said sadly, staring at Adele as she walked away. "I know that something is wrong, and I am going to be here for you. Sooner or later, you will realize that we are all we have now."

†

"Gillian, you look pale, are you feeling alright?" Candice asked concerned.

Gillian swayed slightly and Candice immediately walked over to her and helped her sit down.

"I knew it. You're overdoing it," Candice said as she brushed Gillian's hair from her face.

"I'm just a little tired," Gillian said as she laid back on the small bed. "I haven't been sleeping well."

"I know, sweetheart. Did you take your medication? Do you need me to get you anything?" Candice was unable to hide the concern in her voice.

"No, I just need to close my eyes for a few minutes," Gillian said as her eyes were closing. "Catty…"

"Don't worry about the baby, I'll watch her, okay? You just rest for a bit." Before walking out of the room Candice looked back and saw that Gillian was already fast asleep. She seemed more tired all the time. Gillian would suddenly get pale and would almost faint. As soon as she woke up, Candice would insist that she call the doctor to make sure that everything was okay.

† 

Margot walked into the receiving room and was surprised to see Carlo standing next to the fireplace. He looked so much like her brother when he had been as young as Carlo was now, and just as handsome. She thought he looked just as moody as Matteo had been, too, at that age. God, how Adele had loved him. They had been inseparable, and Matteo had adored her as well. He had always been able to see through her machinations and for that she had always disliked him tremendously. Adele loved her son therefore she would play nicely. At least for now. Afterall, every battle need not be won. Her goal was in being the victor at the end of the war.

"Hello, Carlo." Margot walked up to her nephew and hugged him to her.

"Hello, *Zia* Margot. I'm surprising Mother."

"She should be down for dinner any minute now. How is school?" Margot asked as she walked to the settee and daintily sat down.

"It's all going quite well, thank you. When did you arrive?" Carlo sat down on a wing-backed chair. "How did you find mother?" he asked tentatively.

"She seems…sad." Margot looked down and then up at Carlo. "Gillian…" was all she said, and when she saw the look in Carlos's eyes her suspicions were confirmed. Gillian was gone. And if truth be told Margot was glad it would finally come to an end. Adele had spent too much time on that woman in her opinion.

"Did she tell you?" he asked nervously.

"She didn't have to." Margot played along. "Did she take Catty?"

"Yes, I think my mother is devastated," Carlo said sadly. "I miss them, too."

"Carlo…"

Adele walked into the room at that precise moment.

"Carlo, what a pleasant surprise. *Vieni a baciare tua madre.*" Adele opened her arms to her son.

He quickly got up and went into the warmth of her embrace. "I'm so happy that you have come," Adele said as she held him tightly to her.

Carlo then looked into his mother's eyes. "I am glad I came, too."

"Good, I hope that you are hungry." Adele smiled indulgently.

"He has gotten so tall since the last time I saw him," Margot said as she rose from her seat.

"Yes," Adele said looking from her sister to her son. "He is a man now," she added proudly.

"He will always be your *bambino*," Margot added.

"Yes." Adele's eyes seemed to get sadder.

"Has Catty grown much?" Margot asked innocently.

Carlo immediately turned to her. His eyes showed Margot how unpleased he was with her comment.

"She is getting bigger all the time," Adele said as she turned away from her sister. "Let's go in to dinner. Carlo, *venire*." Adele reached for her son, and they walked towards the dining hall in silence arm in arm.

†

Carlo and Margot sparred over dinner all evening. Carlo was angry at himself because Margot had tricked him into revealing something that his mother obviously was choosing to keep private.

Towards the end of dinner, civility was something that had disappeared. Adele, in the meantime, had been drinking large quantities of wine and had tuned out all the

103

conversation around her. It was night. All that kept going through her mind was that Gillian was with Candice. Where they making love? Was Candice touching her, kissing her? Adele could not control the thoughts that tormented her each night since Gillian had left her. The more she drank, the more distance she felt. She closed her eyes suddenly and just kept them closed.

Carlo said something to her and when she didn't answer, he got up slowly and went to her.

"Come along, Mama," he said gently into her ear. "I'm going to walk you upstairs."

Adele opened her eyes and stared into the eyes of her son. They suddenly filled with tears. "Thank you, *mio caro*. I am rather tired." She tried getting up and failed.

Carlo put his arm around her and helped her up from the chair.

"I know, Mama. When you sleep you will feel better."

"It's late into the evening isn't… why are the nights so long, *mio caro*? Why are the nights so long?" she repeated as she clung to her son.

Margot watched them both and got up and followed them up towards the grand staircase and watched vigilantly as they went up the staircase slowly.

†

Gillian woke up to the darkness and tried getting up slowly.

"Don't, just keep resting," Candice said in the dark.

"Candy?"

"I'm right here."

"Catty?"

"I put her to bed. She is sound asleep, Gilly. I read her a story and she went to sleep."

Candice reached out to her and held her hand. "Lie down, you need your rest."

"I want to see her, Candice." Gillian began to cry. "I want to see my baby," she begged.

"Okay, honey, come on. I'll help you, okay?"

Candice walked over to the other side of the bed and helped Gillian up. She held on to her as Gillian swayed a bit. "Are you really okay?"

"Yes," Gillian answered softly. "I need to see her, please".

"Okay, baby, okay," Candice reassured her.

Slowly they walked into another bedroom. The nightlight was on, and Gillian walked the rest of the way to her daughter's bed on her own. She sat down and lightly caressed the dark locks of hair. Her heart felt the tightness as her little girl turned towards her in her sleep and began to suck her thumb.

Gillian smiled and pulled it out slowly, remembering how Adele would do it and then would indulgently smile at their child. Catty slowly opened her eyes and stared at her mother.

"Is Mama home?" Catty asked softly.

Gillian caressed her face gently. "No, baby."

"I want her." Catty pouted.

"You will see Mama soon, I promise," Gillian answered as she kept caressing the dark locks of her little daughter.

"Sleep with me?"

"Yes, baby, I'm going to sleep with you." Gillian lay down and her daughter instantly filled her arms.

"Night, Mommy," Catty said as she closed her eyes.

"Night, baby." Gillian's eyes closed too as Candice closed the door softly and left the room.

† 

Carlo helped his mother into her bedroom. She sat down on the bed and leaned her head to one of the posts of the bed closest to her.

"Mama…"

"I don't understand, Carlo. I don't understand," Adele said as she looked up to her son.

"Mama, please don't do this to yourself," Carlo said as he sat next to her.

"I don't know what I did. I thought she was happy."
Tears ran down her face.

Carlo placed his hand around hers and squeezed it.

"I don't understand... I don't understand." She shook
her head. "I gave her my world." Adele got up and began to
pace. "How could she do this!"

"Mama, please." Carlo got up as well. "Get some
rest."

"Did she say something to you?" Adele stopped and
stared at him. "Did she!"

"I don't know why she left, Mama. I don't understand
either," Carlo said sadly. "I miss them."

"She will come back," Adele said suddenly. "I will
make her come back."

Carlo looked at her questioning.

"She will come back." She kissed him on the cheek.
"Good night, *mio caro*, go to bed now. All will be well
soon."

"Mama..." Carlo was not sure whether she was just
too drunk or completely building an illusion that somehow,
he knew, would never come to pass. Perhaps once she got
some rest things would seem clearer. He said his goodnight
and left her as she had requested.

†

"Adele…" Margot said softly as she walked into the darkened room. "Adele…"

She had waited most of the night until she thought that her sister would be willing to listen. As she walked into the bedroom her feet tipped over a few bottles. She knelt down and picked up three. Margot smelled the wine that they had once contained.

Gently, she put the bottles on a nearby table. "Adele?"

Margot approached the bed slowly as she heard moaning. "Adele?"

"Gillian…" Adele moaned, mumbling other words.

Margot knew instantly that Adele was beyond comprehending anything at this point as she got closer and closer.

"Gillian, *amore*…come…" Adele pleaded. "*Amore…*"

When Margot reached the side of the bed, she saw Adele's partially naked body sprawled on the bed. Her sleep was tormented as she was obviously calling for Gillian.

Margot leaned down and tried to remove the hair from Adele's forehead. Her hand was suddenly taken, and she was pulled into Adele's embrace. "Gillian…"

Margot pulled away only a bit and looked down at the beauty of Adele's body so close to her. Her hand tentatively touched the softness of the stomach muscles as they twitched when touched.

"Gillian..." Adele moaned again in her drunken stupor.

Margot then leaned down and kissed her soundly on the mouth. "I'm here. Kiss me," she whispered.

"Gillian..." Adele moaned as her lips desperately sought the kiss.

She had felt lips kissing her and as her body had begun to be caressed, the darkness that she had despaired in completely swallowed her into its oblivion.

"Gillian ..." she sobbed in desperation as she completely lost consciousness.

†

"Candice..."

Candice sat up quickly. "What?"

"I need you," Gillian said as she suddenly fell to her knees.

"Oh God." Candice got out of bed and ran to her immediately and dropped to the floor.

"I'm here, baby. I'm here." Candice tried helping her off the floor.

"I need to call the doctor. Oh God, Candice, I hurt so much," Gillian finished saying before her legs gave out beneath her again as she had tried to stand once more.

"Gillian." Candice tried hard to control her emotions.

"I feel sick, help me, I feel like I'm going to be sick."

Candice held her up as she helped her to the bathroom. Gillian was so weak she could barely stand. "I'm going to call an ambulance".

"Call Dr. de Lapandusa, I need him," Gillian managed to say before she started to empty her stomach in the toilet.

Candice held on to her forehead. "I will, baby, as soon as you are doing better. I'm afraid to leave you alone."

Gillian leaned back against the wall closest to her.

"I'm better, call him, Candy, please." Gillian closed her eyes as she leaned her head back. "Call him…"

"Okay, okay, baby. I'll be right back."

Tears rolled down Gillian's cheeks as she whispered, "Dell, I need you so much right now." If only she could feel Adele's arms around her, she would feel better, she kept telling herself. The thought of it, however, only made her cry all the harder.

She covered her mouth as she rushed to the toilet before her stomach began to heave again. Candice rushed back in and knelt down next to her.

"Oh God, baby." She got up and got a wet hand towel and began to wipe Gillian's face as she pulled her head up. "He's on his way. Do you want to try and lay down, Gilly?"

Gillian nodded and leaned on Candice as she helped her walk back into the bedroom.

✝

"Margot, I have been calling you for days!" the male voice said in desperation. "I have been waiting for you."

"Darling, Andrew, I will meet you tomorrow," Margot purred into the phone.

"You said you would contact me as soon as you reached the States!" he insisted.

"Don't be sulky, darling. I will make you glad you waited." Margot opened her robe. She began to caress her body with her free hand. "Mmmm…"

"Margot…"

"I will see you tomorrow, lover, now let me sleep," she said seductively to the man captivated on the other side of the phone. "The things that I will do with you tomorrow will take all of me."

Margot was not surprised by the silence. As planned, all was going to happen as she wished. "Good night, Andrew."

She hung up the receiver then raised her fingers to her nose. "Mmm…nothing will keep me from what I want. God, I love the smell of her."

Margot smiled as she fell asleep remembering all that she had just done.

✝

Candice rushed to the door.

"Good evening. I am Doctor de Lanpandusa. I believe we spoke on the telephone."

"Yes, come in, Doctor, please." Candice let him in and closed the door behind him. "She is having a terrible episode. Please come this way."

"I brought a stronger dose to give her by injection. We are going to have to reevaluate her medication," he said as he followed Candice into the bedroom.

Candice walked up to Gillian's bedside and leaned down. She whispered softly so as not to frighten her any more than she was already. She had known Gillian almost her whole life and she knew that Gillian was scared. She was really scared.

"Gilly, baby, the doctor is here," Candice said softly as she leaned down close to her face.

Gillian's eyes fluttered open and when her eyes met the doctor's eyes a smile appeared slowly. "Hello, Doctor."

"Hello, Mrs. Visconti." He walked up to her as Candice got up and stood to the side, and sat down on the bed. He immediately reached for her wrist and proceeded to take her pulse. "You have been a bad girl haven't you, Gillian." He looked up and regarded the paleness of her face. "I told you that the medicine will take its toll and that you must take care."

"I know, I'm sorry."

He looked up at Candice then back to Gillian in a silent question.

"It's all right, she knows. You can speak in front of her."

The doctor nodded and opened the bag that he had placed on the nightstand when he had sat down.

"I am going to give you a shot to help you along. Gillian, you must slow down, or this will quicken things. Do you understand?" he said gravely to her.

"I will take better care, thank you for coming so quickly."

"I have served the Visconti family for over thirty years. I delivered your daughter. I'm sorry I was the one to have to give you this news," he said sadly as his head bowed.

"You have been my strength. I could not have done this without you. And this is for the best. I count on you to keep your promise to me." Gillian placed her hand lightly on his arm. "It is best for her. You and I both know that."

The doctor looked up sombrely. "Have you decided about the baby?"

"Yes, I won't condemn my child to death upon its birth," she said sadly. "I don't want our baby to suffer such a horrid death," she finished with a sob.

"I will make the arrangements." He looked away and reached for the syringe.

"There is no chance for my baby, is there?" She knew the answer before she asked.

"I'm sorry, Gillian, none." He proceeded to give her the injection without looking at her. "Babies born with the virus seldom last long and the short life they have is filled with horrible pain till their last breath," he said mercilessly.

"Does it have to be so soon?" she asked as she placed a hand on her abdomen protectively.

"The sooner you do it the more strength you can count on. Later on, it will take too much from you. I will make the arrangement and get in touch with you," he said as he began to put his instruments back into his bag.

"She must never know. I don't want her to ever know," Gillian said, holding back another sob as she reached for his arm for solace.

"I will never tell her," he assured her as he looked down at her hand over his arm.

"And you are sure that she does not have it...?"

"I am sure Gillian; Adele does not have it. She was lucky..." he finished saying as he looked away.

"Thank you." Gillian said softly.


"I will let you rest now. It will take a few days before you have all your strength back. I want to see you again then, unless you have another episode. We will see about the arrangement then, all right?"

"All right. Thank you, be there for her when..."

"Rest now." He patted her hand lightly, got up, and followed Candice out the door.

114

†

Candice let the doctor out and instead of going back to Gillian she walked up to the glass wall of the expansive living room. Something inside her just needed time to digest it all. No matter how she thought about it and turned it around and around, she could not just forget it. And it hurt so very much that sometimes the pain of knowing was unbearable, like now. She had to be strong. This was her chance, her time with the woman that had taken her heart and had held it for most of her life. Gillian was dying. Her Gillian was dying. Candice's head bowed down as her body began to shake with the sobbing. Gillian was dying and there was nothing she could do to stop it.

†

Adele's eyes opened slowly. The light coming through the curtains was causing her headache to grow in magnitude. She tried sitting up slowly and felt a terrible ache all over her body. Her muscles felt like lead as she leaned towards the backboard and her head throbbed.

"Oh God, I feel like death," Adele mumbled. She tried getting up and sat down again quickly as she felt a sharp pain between her legs. Adele gritted her teeth and groaned. Her whole body ached.

She felt a light knock on the door before it opened.

"Good morning," said Margot as she walked in. "Or maybe I should say good afternoon."

"In the name of God, Margot, please speak softly. My head feels like it's going to fall off," Adele said as she clung to the bedpost.

"Let me help you." Margot approached her slowly.

Adele tried pulling the sheet to cover her nakedness.

"Here." Margot helped cover her.

"Thank you," Adele said as she looked at her sister.

Margot caressed her face softly. "I'm going to run your bath and then I will help you get in it," she said as she was walking towards the bathroom.

"Why are you doing this, Margot?" Adele could not keep the sarcasm from her voice.

"Because you need it. Because I'm your sister and because I think you need me right now," she said simply. She continued walking into the bathroom, leaving Adele to think about the words that her sister had unexpectedly said. They had never been close. From her earliest memories, Margot had not been present in her life and when she was, it was with disdain not love.

Adele heard the water running and again just let her head lean on the post of the bed. She closed her eyes, trying to come to some kind of control over her body that refused to cooperate.

Suddenly she felt a light touch on her arm and her eyes opened to her sister in front of her.

"Come, let me take care of you. Just this once let me do that," Margot implored.

Adele's head nodded and allowed her sister to help her up and walk her to the tub.

"How much wine did you drink?" Margot asked as she helped guide her into the bathroom. She tried pulling the sheet away, but Adele held onto it.

"Come on, I will help you into the tub. Come on, let's go," Margot insisted gently, Adele let go of the sheet as Margot helped her into it.

"Mmm…that feels good," Adele said as she closed her eyes and leaned her head back.

Margot watched her hungrily from just a few feet away.

†

"Are you feeling better?" Candice asked as she walked in with a tray followed by Catty.

"Hi, Mommy," Catty said as she got into bed with her mother.

"I'm feeling much better, thank you." She smiled at Candice and then turned to her daughter. "Good morning, sweet pea."

Catty giggled and snuggled next to her mother on the bed.

"I brought my two favourite ladies breakfast in bed," Candice said as she placed the tray over Gillian's legs as she sat up.

"That is so kind of you." Gillian met Candice's eyes and smiled. "I don't know what I would do without you."

"You don't have to find out. I am here. I love you," Candice said softly as she looked towards Catty. She didn't want to see how Gillian's eyes would react to the words she had just voiced.

She was surprised when she felt Gillian's hand on hers. Candice looked up and found the tenderness she had always seen in those eyes and for now that was everything.

"Mommy, juice please," Catty said sweetly. Both women smiled and began to eat the breakfast in front of them.

†

"Why are you really here, Margot?" Adele asked as she lay in the tub. Her head was still leaning back, and her eyes had remained closed.

"Because I don't want…"

Adele opened her eyes and tried sitting up a little as she saw Margot turn away from her. She waited for Margot to formulate an answer.

"I don't want to feel alone anymore... And I think that you are lonely, too." Margot turned around with tear-filled eyes. "You are part of me. I want to love you. I want you to know that I will be there if you need me."

Adele said nothing as she searched her face. The words had surprised her. She and Margot had always had a strange relationship. They had been more strangers than sisters for the past few years, and after Matteo had died, she had to admit that she had considered reaching out to Margot as well. But Gillian had soothed the pain of losing her beloved twin brother and somehow building a relationship with Margot always seemed... What did she feel about her sister? There was something about Margot that she didn't understand, something that had always kept them at arm's length.

Margot had been twelve when she and Matteo were born. Her mother, Angelina Adele Masaretti, had married Sir George Lancaster, an English gentleman who, in the end, had no great fortune, possessing only his title. Angelina gave birth to Margot and refused to provide the male heir that Sir Lancaster so dearly desired. He was madly in love with his Italian wife, but ten years later he was replaced in her affections by her next prospect, Conte Vittorio Visconti de Caravagio.

Angelina divorced her English Lord and married her Italian Count before the year's end. Matteo and Adele were born six months after their marriage. Victor as Vittorio was called was very much enamoured with her and madly in love with his children. Angelina had given him a son and a daughter. He lavished extravagant gifts on her and was generous with Margot, his stepdaughter, as well. Unfortunately, Victor was killed while flying one of his airplanes, leaving his young children the heirs to one of the greatest fortunes in Italy. The stipulation was simple, blood always inherited blood. Wives in his family were left an allowance but children were the ones that inherited.

Margot, along with their mother, seemed to be living in luxury but had very little means to truly spend. In time, Angelina began to look for other prospects and Margot, upon her twentieth birthday noticed her beautiful sister.

†

*"This piece of cake is specially for you."* Margot had handed the young Adele a plate.

*"But the first piece is for the birthday person,"* Adele replied, surprised.

*"It pleases me that you should have it."* Margot smiled and was pleased to see the smile on her sister's lips.

*"Thank you,"* Adele said as she took the plate.

*"You are welcome. Do I get a kiss?"*

*Adele kissed her older sister and began to eat her cake. She never noticed the look of malice that was reflected in Margot's eyes.*

†

Adele remembered the times that she had looked up to her big sister. Margot had been her hero. Margot would spoil her and take her to the park. Margo would sneak ice cream up to her room when their mother would despair of her antics and would send her to bed without dessert. She had loved Margot until Margot had told her mother about a girl that Adele had feelings for. She had trusted Margot with this knowledge and the betrayal of that trust had always been there between them. Adele's mother had reacted by striking her daughter over and over as Adele defiantly stood her ground. This was the point in which her mother saw the strength that she would not ever win over as she stared at the blood smeared face of her daughter.

It was also by that time that Adele also felt that there was something about Margot that had made her feel uncomfortable, something that made her want to keep her at a distance, but Margot had also been the older sister she had always counted on. There were times that Adele caught her staring at her, and her skin began to crawl, and that is when the distance had begun to grow between them. That had been the defining moment of their relationship. Something had told her to stay away, and she had. She didn't need Margot; she had her beloved brother, Matteo. Matteo was the other part of her; they had always been like the Yin and Yang. Matteo was fun but Matteo was also her protector and she adored him. He was her older brother she told herself with a giggle, after all he was a whole minute older. It had always been the standing joke between them. How she missed him; he had loved her to the very end, and she had known that even after his death with the gift he had unknowingly left for her.

Adele saw as Margot then turned to her. "I can't change the past, Adele, I can only wish that you and I were close again. You know I love you. It is time that you forgive me and let me be here for you. I know that Gillian is gone." Margot saw the pain immediately register in Adele's eyes. "I'm so very sorry."

Adele looked away as her eyes filled with tears she could not control from falling. And it took them both by surprise when Adele's body began to shake as she sobbed and covered her face. She could no longer control the anguish inside her. Her heart was breaking and nothing would ever make it heal.

Margot went to her and held her. She was surprised when Adele's arms went out to her and clung to her as she wept. Adele clung to her in desperation. Margot began to caress her hair. "It will be alright. I'm here to hold you. It will be alright." She kissed Adele's head and closed her eyes in ecstasy as she held her sister closer to her.

†

Adele walked up to the limousine as it pulled up in front of the house.

The back door opened unceremoniously as her daughter ran out and filled her arms.

"Mama, Mama!"

Adele picked her up and held her tightly to her.

"I missed you, my *principesa,*" she said as she buried her face in her daughter's hair. She took in the sweet smell of her little girl. At that moment she realized how much her soul ached as she held her precious child to her, and she smiled with joy.

Gillian then got out slowly and Adele's eyes immediately locked with hers.

"Good morning, Gillian," Adele said as she put her daughter down gently.

"Mama." Catty pulled at her mother's hand.

"Yes, darling?" Adele looked down at their daughter indulgently.

"I don't want you to go away anymore," Catty said to her mother.

Adele looked towards Gillian who seemed confused as well.

"I haven't gone anywhere, darling. I'm right here," Adele said as she knelt down in front of her daughter.

"I want you and Mommy, don't go away anymore." Catty put her little arms around Adele's neck.

123

Adele's eyes filled with tears as she stood up, holding her daughter tightly to her. Her eyes became black chips of accusation at Gillian who looked away sadly.

Adele walked into the house with Catty in her arms as Gillian walked in behind her.

Adele gave all her attention to Catty as Margot came down the staircase and walked towards Gillian.

"Hello, Gillian," Margot said as she kissed her lightly on both cheeks.

"Hello, Margot," Gillian said as she looked towards Adele. She wasn't sure how Adele wanted to handle this, so she looked towards her for guidance. Adele picked up their daughter and walked over to her, placed her arm around her waist and kissed her lightly on the lips.

Gillian looked up into the eyes that were familiar and held only love for her. How easy it had always been to simply just drown in them and love her. Adele had never denied her love; she had never shied from showing her in front of others; and now this farce, because it surely now was a farce, hurt her to know that she would never truly see that love in those dark eyes again.

"Hello, Kateryna," Margot said as she sought to caress her niece.

Catty turned away from her and buried her face in her mother's neck.

†

"She is tired, Margot. I'm sure she will be better behaved once she has had her nap," Adele explained simply. The truth of the matter was that Catty had never been receptive to her aunt's attention.

"She has grown since I last saw her." Margot directed her smile to Adele and totally ignored Gillian.

Margot was being intentionally rude, and Adele immediately reacted to it. Gillian was her wife and as such she would be respected in her house. Just as quickly, she also knew that Gillian wasn't really that anymore. Gillian lived, loved, and slept with someone else. That one last thought suddenly filled her body with an ache that she could not bear. It hurt. It hurt more than she would have ever imagined. The pain seemed to grow with time rather than lessen. She felt tired. She wanted to just take her wife and child somewhere far away and live the dream that she once thought would never end.

"Gillian, darling, you look rather pale, not like yourself at all." Margot's tone was venomous.

"I'm…" Gillian's eyes began to fill with tears. Margot had always been unkind to her, and at times she had actually been cruel, but never in front of Adele. She could feel Adele's body stiffen next to her.

"Come along, *cara*, you must be tired after your trip," Adele said a bit too curtly, staring at her sister. Gillian nodded and Adele guided both mother and daughter up the staircase as Margot glared after them.

Adele's behaviour had surprised her. Now she wasn't sure exactly what was going on. They walked up the staircase with their daughter as if nothing had changed.

†

Adele put down her daughter and sat down next to her on the bed. Catty rubbed her eyes, and a small yawn escaped her mouth as her mother adoringly looked at her.

"You are tired, little one." Adele caressed her child's hair and leaned down and placed a soft kiss on her forehead. As she raised her face very close to her daughter's face she whispered, "Welcome home, my sweet one."

†

Gillian was putting away some of Catty's clothes but could not help being pulled into the love being displayed in front of her. Adele had always managed to fascinate her at times like this. This was the woman that she loved and the one that she had to stay away from. Adele would never have left her even under the circumstances that she found herself in. She would have stuck by her till the very end, risking getting the disease. Adele would survive this only if she gave her some solid ground to hang onto. She had to do this even if it meant that she had to make Adele hate her. If she could kill at least a part of Adele's love for her that would be enough. Adele would go on for their daughter's sake.

Gillian was suddenly filled with a longing that she could barely control. She wanted to run to Adele and seek the comfort she so dearly craved from her lover's embrace. She shut her eyes and tried pulling herself away from what she so desperately craved. Suddenly she heard a whisper close to her ear like in a faraway dream.

†

"Do you need a nap too, cara mia?" Adele asked softly.

Gillian could not control a smile from appearing as her eyes remained closed. All her body knew was that Adele was close.

Adele had walked over to Gillian after putting the baby to bed and felt Gillian lean back against her and was surprised but allowed it. Gillian's body felt warm as it leaned back against her own and suddenly her senses were filled with the fragrance of Gillian's hair. Adele closed her eyes, trying desperately not to reach out and embrace her. Then without a thought, her arms surrounded the body that melded into hers just as Gillian began to collapse.

"What?" Adele was trying to hold Gillian up, not understanding what was happening. Somehow, she managed to get them both to the floor without Gillian hurting herself. "Gillian... Gillian." Adele caressed her lover's face softly as

127

her emotions ran rampant from confusion and fear. She looked towards Catty's bed and saw that she was fast asleep.

†

*"Come take a nap with me, cara mia," Adele whispered into her ear.*

*"Dell, it's two o'clock in the afternoon," Gillian teased, knowing full well that the last thing her lover had in mind was sleeping.*

*Adele pulled her back against her. "I will always want you, cara," she finished saying while kissing Gillian's ear. "Our little principessa is taking a nap and my body aches for you, cara mia. Come to bed with me..."*

*Gillian turned around in her arms and saw the molten desire apparent in the eyes of Adele. She raised her hand to caress the face of the woman that she loved with her whole heart.*

*"I have never felt love as I feel for you," Gillian said with such emotion that Adele pulled back a little and looked at her. "I cannot imagine living without you."*

*Adele took her into her embrace and held her tightly. "Mi amore, my life will end the day I lose you. I will die with you. Gillian, I love you more than life itself."*

*Gillian pulled away and saw as tears ran down the beautiful face of her Contessa as she said, "You are my life.*

*During it I will love no other. After you I shall simply die."*
*Adele stared deeply into her eyes as she had said the words.*

*Gillian brushed the tears away. "I plan to live forever in this fairytale with you, my dark-haired lover. I want a hundred years, at the very least." Gillian smiled.*

*"One year, one day or even one minute... I would give up my life to spend it with you," Adele said seriously.*

*Gillian smiled. "Let's not speak of sad things. We have a lifetime in front of us. And..."*

*"And?" Adele asked.*

*"And, I want my nap," Gillian said as she met Adele's lips with her own.*

*That afternoon Adele had loved her; loved her slowly, with great tenderness and with such passion that it had surprised her somehow. Later as they lay in each other's arms she felt Adele's embrace tighten around her. She looked up and found those dark eyes that had bewitched her staring at her.*

*"What is it, darling?" Gillian asked as her hand caressed Adele's face softly.*

*"If I ever lose you, I will die," Adele said as a tear escaped from her eye and rolled down her cheek.*

*"You will never die, my love, you will never lose me." Gillian kissed her lips as Adele's arms embraced her and made love to her once more that sunny afternoon as their daughter slept safely close by.*

†

Gillian's eyes opened slowly and the throbbing pain in her head was unbearable. A moan escaped her lips and Adele seemed to be immediately next to her. Gillian felt disoriented and overwhelmed with the searing spasms of pain.

"Don't try to get up, *cara*," Adele said softly.

"My head, it hurts…" The pain was so intense she began to cry and was instantly taken into a warm embrace. Gillian shut her eyes and buried her face into the softness of Adele's arms.

Gillian clung to her for comfort as she wept. She slowly started to relax as Adele methodically caressed her hair and whispered phrases of love in Italian to her. Gillian's body began to surrender to the warmth and safety of the embrace that held her. Something inside her had needed this as gradually her senses gave in to sleep just as she had done many times before in Adele's arms. And this her body took in; how could she give this up? This sense of safety and warmth. But, for now she needed Adele, she needed this to go on another day. And this surrender brought her the peace she needed to find the sleep that had escaped her.

Adele leaned back slowly taking Gillian's body with her. She could feel Gillian's arms clinging to her even in her sleep. At that moment she refused to think. The pain inside her was now bearable. Adele simply held Gillian closer to her and closed her own eyes as well.

†

"What is the commotion, Marco?" Margot asked irritably.

"Mrs. Visconti fainted, and the Contessa had me call the doctor to come and see her." Marco could not hide the concern from his face.

"Fainted? Is that all? Seriously, Adele does overreact over things," Margot said as she walked away leaving Marco surprised.

At that moment the phone rang, and Margot listened. The doctor was at the gate. She would wait and go up with him.

Margot and the doctor walked towards the bed and Marco lingered behind to make sure that he was not needed.

As Margot reached the bed she was presented with both Adele and Gillian sleeping peacefully in a lover's embrace. Something inside her began to boil. This was not what she had expected to find.

"Adele?" Margot said loud enough to rouse the two sleeping lovers.

Adele automatically tightened her hold on Gillian who began to pull away as she was awakened.

"Margot…you've awakened her." Adele tried to control her irritation.

†

Gillian pulled away slowly out of Adele's embrace and as her eyes began to focus, she saw Dr. de Lanpandusa looking back at her.

"Doctor?" Gillian asked in confusion.

Gillian was about to speak when she felt a warm liquid begin to drip from her nose.

"*Cara*…you're bleeding!" Adele said as she reached out for Gillian.

"What?" Gillian brought her hand up after wiping her nose and stared at the blood on it. When she saw Adele reaching out for her, she pushed her away harshly. "Stay away!"

Adele was taken aback from Gillian's reaction.

"I am only trying to…"

"Just stay away from me!" Gillian said aggressively. "Go! I don't want you! What do I have to do to get that through your head? Leave me alone!"

Adele stared at her for a moment, both sets of eyes locked. The distance that only a moment before had not existed was solid and in place in Gillian's eyes. They were no longer one.

Adele got up and faced the doctor. "See to my wife. I would like to talk to you later down in the library." She then simply just walked out of the room with Margot close behind her.

The doctor was immediately next to her. "Gillian, if you don't listen to me this will happen again, and every time after you will be weaker and weaker." He put gloves on and began to clean the blood off her face gently.

"I…I'm so frightened," Gillian said miserably. "I was afraid that she would touch me."

"I know. She didn't." The doctor tried to remain detached and yet how could one not feel for the plight that the beautiful woman in front of him was fighting so valiantly. He had to try harder to remain detached. "You did the right thing, of course."

Gillian looked up with tear filled eyes. "Even now she wants me."

"I could see that, Mrs. Visconti," he said sadly. "It might be better if you do not stay here for a few days. You are going to be bleeding like this on and off for the next few days."

"My daughter?" Gillian said close to tears.

"It might be best if you have some distance from her right now as well." He looked away not wanting to see the pain his words were producing to the woman in front of him.

"What will you say to her?"

"I will simply tell her that you are just under stress."

Gillian looked down at her hands. "Just touching her with my blood I might have infected her, wouldn't I, Doctor?" Her eyes begged for him to disprove her words.

"Yes, Gillian, it might." He answered her without looking away. "We don't know enough about this to be sure...blood and shared fluids you must be cautious of not sharing."

Gillian looked away as tears ran down her face freely. "Just for a moment when I was in her arms, I ..."

"You what, Gillian?" he inquired tenderly.

"I thought that this was just a horrible dream. I don't want this for her. I..." Gillian covered her eyes as she wept.

"All I can do is try to make you as comfortable as I can, Gillian, in hope that some type of treatment is found. I know how hard this is for you. I know how hard the next few weeks will be." He saw her eyes turn to him.

"You scheduled it, didn't you?" she asked, knowing too well what the answer would be.

"One week from today and, in view of this, it is appropriate."

She stared at him unable to speak as she felt a pain in her chest spread within her.

"It is the right thing, Gillian. This child would only know pain and death. In the four years since its discovery, this AIDS virus has killed thousands and we still don't completely understand how it works. There are hundreds of babies in the city alone that have been born with AIDS and who are living without any hope for a future. You are doing the right thing, my dear." He covered her hand and squeezed it.

Her eyes filled with tears yet again as her head nodded. "I know. It hurts so much to know that this baby is inside me and it will never have a chance to...she will never know this child. It was going to be a surprise..." Gillian trailed off and smiled sadly. "We both wanted another baby so much."

"I'm sorry, my dear. I'm so very sorry."

†

Adele went into the library and straight for the decanters near the window. She poured herself a full tumbler of scotch. As she raised the glass to her mouth, she suddenly threw it across the room. The amber liquid spread everywhere.

"Fuck!" Adele roared as the glass had mashed into a million pieces. "Fuck!" she yelled again in frustration.

Margot, who had been following close behind, froze by the door.

Adele turned towards her aggressively. "What are you looking at?"

Margot said nothing as Adele started at her enraged.

Adele turned around and with one clean swipe cleared the server nearby of all the decanters. She didn't move for a moment as she leaned with her palms supporting herself on the table.

Marco suddenly appeared next to Margot.

"Is everything alright…" He stopped himself as he took in the scene before him.

Margot turned to him. "Everything is fine, please arrange for this room to be cleaned up."

He only hesitated for a moment and when Adele said nothing, he left to make sure that the task was done.

Margot walked slowly towards her sister and when she stood mere inches away, she waited for a moment before her hand touched Adele's shoulder tentatively. Adele jerked her shoulder to shrug her away. Margot waited a moment and tried again. This time Adele turned into her embrace. Margo held her tightly as Adele's sobbing racked her body while she clung to Margot in desperation.

†

Dr. de Lanpandusa was led into one of the many receiving rooms of the house. He looked around the mahogany panels that encased the room. He walked in slowly taking all the hues of blue and gold of the silks that covered the windows, he now realized what it was when people said it smelled like money, he was surrounded with its trappings. When his eyes turned towards the side Margot

136

immediately got up from the settee, she was sitting on to receive him.

"Hello, Doctor, please come in and sit down." Margo's voice was like a soft purr.

He was about to walk towards her when he stopped himself as he caught the sight of Adele nearby.

Adele remained standing by a nearby window staring out as he entered the room.

"How is Mrs. Visconti?" Margot asked as she gestured for him to sit.

"Thank you," he said as he sat down. "She seems to be under a great deal of stress..." he trailed off as Adele turned to face him and crossed her arms. Her eyes seemed to be made of cold black granite. Dr de Lanpandusa waited silently for the woman in front of him to speak. As he waited, he began to take in the obvious signs of stress evident in Adele herself. She had lost weight and the dark circles under her eyes were signals that she had not been sleeping.

"Please continue," Adele finally said.

"She needs rest; perhaps a holiday."

"A holiday," Adele said as she turned around and walked back towards the place she had been standing before. Suddenly her shoulders seemed to droop, and she looked weary. Her right hand ran through her hair and the doctor noticed the way it was shaking. She seemed tired and defeated when she turned directly towards them again.

"Thank you, doctor; Margot will see you out." She left them alone as she went up the staircase.

†

Adele walked up the staircase slowly. Every step took more and more out of her. She walked into the bedroom that she had left Gillian in without knocking.

Gillian looked up, then quickly looked away. She didn't trust herself with Adele. Her emotions were too raw; she felt too vulnerable and all that she could think of was that she wanted Adele's arms around her again.

"The doctor tells me that you are reacting to stress." Adele looked at Gillian who said nothing in return. Adele walked closer to Gillian and sat down in a nearby chair. "The doctor suggests a holiday."

"I called Candice. She will be coming for me. Will you keep Catty for a few days?" Gillian never raised her eyes.

Adele got up slowly a minute later. "Our daughter will never need permission to stay at her home. You can return to her when you like," she said curtly as she walked out of the room.

Gillian looked up to see her walk out and close the door behind her. Never could she have imagined Adele's desire even now for reconciliation. Gillian cried all the harder. Her once-upon-a-time indomitable lover was willing and obviously desired her back under any circumstances.

Adele had humbled herself over and over again. Her pride, that was so much a part of her, had left her. The thought of her once proud Contessa reduced to tears, asking her to stay, was breaking her heart.

"Dell," she said softly as tears ran down her face. "I'm sorry, darling. I'm so very sorry. I'm doing this for you, Dell. This is for you, my love. I don't want this for you."

†

"Mother, I'm not sure yet," Margot said in exasperation.

"Is she gone for good?"

"I don't know. Be patient, Mother. This will end, I promise you that," Margot said with conviction to her mother over the telephone.

"And Adele..."

"This is for the best," Margot replied. "We must think of Carlo, Mother. It is only right that he takes Matteo's place. He is your only legitimate grandchild."

Once reminded of her beloved dead son, her mother had responded as Margot expected she would.

"You are right, of course. Adele is obsessed with that woman. Carlo is the only legitimate heir. Kateryna is not our blood," she stated with conviction.

"Goodbye mother; I'll call you very soon." Margot hung up and smiled.

†

"Are you feeling better?" Candice asked as she sat on the side of the bed.

"Much better. How long have I been sleeping?" Gillian tried sitting up further.

"Twelve hours."

"That long?" Gillian asked surprised.

"You were pretty wiped out, honey."

Gillian then suddenly looked incredibly sad as she looked into Candice's eyes.

Candice placed her hand on hers.

"What is it, Gilly?"

"Next week…" Gillian said all choked up.

"What, honey? What next week?" Candice urged her to answer gently.

"My baby, my baby will be gone." Gillian broke into tears as Candice took her in her arms.

†

"Hey, kiddo." Carlo greeted his little sister.

When Catty saw him, she ran into her big brother's arms. He lifted her up in the air and she broke out in giggles.

"Hello," said the nanny as she walked up to them.

"Hello. I'll stay with her."

"Very well, sir."

The young woman walked back into the house to prepare them something to eat for when they finished playing. It was evident to everyone that Carlo adored his little sister.

"How is the most beautiful princess in the whole wide world?"

"Okay." She giggled and gifted him with the brightest smile he had ever seen. From the moment his mother placed her into his arms she had taken hold of his heart as her small little hand wrapped itself around his finger.

They played in the garden for over an hour, unaware that Adele looked at them from her bedroom window.

Carlo sat down and leaned back against a large tree trunk. His little sister sat on his lap and leaned her head against his chest. He hugged her closer to him and kissed her on the top of her dark curls.

Adele looked at her children and again asked herself for the millionth time what had gone wrong. She walked over to the bed that Gillian and she had shared if only for a few hours the day before. Her arms ached for the woman that they had held. Her hand gently caressed the pillow. Adele then lay down and put her face on the pillow and wept. "Gillian…" And again her mind was filled with memories that continued to keep her a prisoner.

✝

*"Why are you being so stubborn?"* Gillian asked in exasperation.

*"This is who I am, Gillian."* Adele tried walking away. She felt Gillian's hand on her arm holding her in place and she turned towards her.

*"Not anymore, I'm in your life now. Some things we have to decide together. This will affect Carlo and our baby."* Gillian went into her arms.

Adele was left speechless. Her arms went around Gillian and at that moment their daughter chose to kick; Adele smiled and something inside her just let go.

*"I'm sorry...be patient with me, Tesoro mio,"* Adele said softly as she kissed her lover on the temple. *"I am too..."*

Gillian pulled away just a little and smiled at her lover.

*"I'm too arrogant and too proud,"* Adele said softly. She then looked down and caressed Gillian's belly.

*"I know. I don't want to change you. I just want to be a real part of your life, nothing else will do."* Gillian caressed her cheek and kissed Adele's lips lightly.

*"I love you, cara mia. You must know that; nothing will ever change that,"* Adele assured her passionately.

Gillian's hands went up on either side of Adele's face. *"I know that darling."*

*"I'm difficult, yes?"*

*"Yes, but you are worth it." Gillian leaned closer as Adele pulled her into an ardent kiss. At that moment Adele pulled away and they both laughed as their daughter had once again let her presence be known with a swift kick.*

*"Your daughter, darling, wants attention." Gillian laughed as she caressed her belly.*

*"Stubborn." Adele smiled at her lover.*

*"Just like her beautiful mother."*

†

"Margot, I want to see you."

"Yes, darling, you have been so good. I will be there tonight," Margot purred into the phone.

"You will come, won't you, Margot? I need to see you…"

"I am going to be with you all night."

"I don't know if I can spend all night…" He hesitated.

"Then go to that mousy wife of yours!" Margot spat.

"No, dearest, nothing matters, the only thing that matters is our being together," he cajoled her.

"Remember that. You know how much you like what I do for you, and the things that I will do to you." Margot laughed. "You haven't changed your mind, have you? You want me, don't you?"

"Yes, come tonight. No, I haven't changed my mind. I will do whatever you want just come," he begged.

"Till tonight then..." she said as she hung up the phone.

†

"This is 1990! You're telling me that there is nothing that can be done?" Candice asked in desperation. "Don't they have experimental drugs? Anything is better than what she is going through." She sat down deflated.

"I understand how you feel, Ms. Wentz. Time will find a cure for this disease. Unfortunately, time is what we don't have," said Dr. de Lanpandusa patiently as he sat across from Candice.

"I don't know how she does it," Candice said sadly with her head bowed. "Everything that she loves... and yes, I know she loves Adele Visconti."

The doctor said nothing as she looked up angrily.

"She doesn't know I'm here. Look, I don't know about all this. Adele would make this so much more bearable for her. I...love her. I can't stand to see her like this," Candice said desperately.

"I know that you love Gillian but, this is what Gillian wants. Has it occurred to you that having Adele close to her might create even more stress for her? She would be worrying about so much more." The doctor tried to reason with her.

Candice said nothing. Gillian seemed to be getting worse and, at this point, she was willing to do anything, even bring Adele to her.

"In maybe five, ten years...time is what we need. I can only try to keep her alive...if she has this child, we may lose her. And what kind of life can an infant with AIDS have? Most babies last a few months. Maybe a year and the death is ugly, Ms. Wentz. Is that what you want for her if she even survives the birth?

Candice said nothing as she got up. "Thank you for seeing me. I love her. I just thought..."

The doctor looked at her sympathetically. "I can see that you do. Make sure she is there, please."

Candice nodded and walked out, broken hearted for Gillian.

# Chapter Eight

---

Adele was over Gillian as they were both undulating in overwhelming passion. Gillian threw her head back as she arched her back. "Dell, now...please."

Adele slid two fingers into her as her mouth claimed a hardened nipple and sucked on it forcefully.

"Ohhh..." Gillian began to pant as she felt the tide of the orgasm getting closer. Adele added a third finger and began to pump harder in syncopated rhythm with her mouth feasting on Gillian's nipple. They were both suddenly panting harder and harder as they both came together, almost by agreement.

*They lay spent holding each other. A cool breeze came through the opened window and caressed their bodies covered with the sheen that lovemaking left on their skin.*

*"I love you," whispered Adele in her ear, holding her tighter.*

*Gillian buried her face in Adele's neck and kissed it. "I love you, too. Promise to bring me back to this beautiful place on our next anniversary."*

*"I'm so glad that you like this island, cara. I have always loved coming here," Adele said into her hair. "Gillian..."*

*"Yes, darling?"*

*"Happy anniversary. I bought us this house a week ago," Adele said mischievously.*

*Gillian got up suddenly on one elbow and stared at Adele.*

*"It's yours, cara. We can come whenever you like." Adele leaned closer and kissed her lightly on the lips. "No one will know of this place, only you and me."*

*"No one?" Gillian asked seriously.*

*"No one, cara mia. No entourage, no outside world, this is just for you and me and our family," said Adele seriously. "I love you, Gillian. I am keeping my promise to you. This is our world and our world alone."*

*Gillian went into Adele's arms. "I love you, Dell, God, how I love you."*

*"Happy anniversary, cara mia…" And Adele sealed her words with kisses that led to their love making.*

✝

Adele woke up slowly. She felt like everything ached. It was like her subconscious fought against her waking and bringing her back from happiness into the pain that now was a constant in her world and in her body.

She covered her eyes to keep the light out. Every moment of every day her desolation grew. Gillian's voice, her presence, was so needed that Adele knew that time would never truly cure even a portion of her need.

And as life often does, her need was answered as the phone beside her bed rang.

"Hello," Adele said softly. Something inside her knew who the caller would be.

"Hello, Dell," said Gillian on the other end.

"Are you feeling better?" Adele asked with genuine concern.

Suddenly they seemed cocooned. The distance served its purpose, and they could be more themselves.

"Yes, I am."

"I…" Adele's voice became deep with emotion.

"I need you to understand," Gillian said sadly.

"What do you want me to understand, *cara*, that you don't love me anymore?" There was no anger in Adele's voice as she said this.

There was an audible intake of breath from Gillian. "Help me, please. You have always been the stronger one," Gillian said as she wept. "Will you, darling? Will you help me?"

There was silence for a moment. Adele found herself unable to reply, when she was about to speak. "*Cara...*" she stopped when she heard Candice speaking in the background.

"Hi baby, are you feeling better?" Candice said as she walked in and kissed Gillian on the cheek.

"Yes, thank you," Gillian answered and turned back to her phone call. "Dell?"

The phone tone changed, and she realized that Adele had hung up. A tear slid down the cheek of each woman on either end of the phone.

†

It had been close to two weeks since Adele and Gillian had seen or spoken to one another.

"Contessa, here is your itinerary for the week. I confirmed the ones in red and made arrangements for the benefit on Friday," Gloria Betancourt, Adele's personal assistant, pointed out. "Will you and Mrs. Visconti require any other reservations such as for the salon as you have previously?"

"What is this benefit for again?" Adele finally seemed to pay attention.

"It's for the wing of the children's ward at St. Anthony's Hospital." Gloria was surprised. Adele was always so in tune with her engagements. "You are one of the sponsors of this event and will be handing them a check for one million dollars."

"Yes, of course." Adele looked away suddenly and Gloria waited silently. "Please leave me for about five minutes, Gloria. We can resume when I finish this call I have to make."

"Of course, Contessa." Gloria walked out without another word.

Adele picked up the receiver and began to dial.

"Hello?" Gillian's voice rushed inside her as it came through the telephone.

"Gillian…"

"Dell? I wanted to…"

"Gillian." Adele cut her off immediately. "There is a benefit this Friday for the children's ward at St. Anthony's Hospital. The Caravagio Foundation will be giving them a substantial donation. This was something you wanted. I want you with me that night. They will expect us both to attend." Adele delivered the very businesslike speech. The fact that it was totally without emotion was not lost on Gillian.

"Friday?"

"Yes, is this too short of a notice for you?" Adele began to allow the sarcasm to seep in. "You will have to change your plans, Gillian." Adele left no room for argument.

"All right, Dell," Gillian said wearily. "How is Catty?"

"She has been spending time with Carlo."

"Is Carlo home?" The tenderness in Gillian's voice came through.

"He arrived over a week ago," Adele said curtly. She wanted to avoid playing these scenes with Gillian that only left her feeling more pain then the usual.

"How is he? Did he make the lacrosse team?"

"Why do you care?" Adele was unable to control the anger in her voice at this point. "What does it matter to you what my son does?"

"Because he is not only yours, he is mine, too, and I love him." Gillian's voice was full of emotion. "I want to know about him."

"You have destroyed my home and tried to take my daughter from me. I will not allow you to bewitch my son. Stay away from Carlo, do you hear me!" Adele was yelling at the top of her lungs now. "Damn you to hell!"

"Dell…"

"Enough!" Adele waited as the silence between them grew.

"I don't want him to think that I don't love him, Dell," Gillian insisted. She wanted to at least be able to have limited access to Carlo. They had both gotten very close after the initial clash. She and Carlo had grown to love each other. Gillian never missed a game at his school. She was the one that the school called, and she was the one that was there when Adele was off closing some deal halfway around the world.

"Where would he get the idea that you just stop loving people that you profess to love forever?" Adele allowed the venom to pour over every word.

"Dell, don't let this situation between us touch our children." Gillian tried to appeal to her sensibilities.

"You are the one that has created this, Gillian, not I. Now, when will you be home?" Adele refused to play her game.

"Thursday."

"Gloria will be making the usual appointments for the benefit." Adele quickly went back to her business mode. "I will have her copy you. Goodbye, Gillian."

"Goodbye, Dell," Gillian said sadly.

†

"Can I go in with her?" Candice asked Doctor de Lanpandusa.

"It will be better if you don't."

"She's so upset, Doctor. She won't stop crying." Candice's tears ran down her face. "I'm afraid for her."

The doctor was about to say something and seemed to stop himself.

"Please, let me be there with her. It will make it easier for her," Candice begged.

"All right, Ms. Wentz." He turned and headed towards one of the operating rooms of the private clinic.

Candice went back into the waiting room where Gillian was getting ready for her procedure.

When Candice walked in, she found Gillian sitting on a gurney with a hospital gown on. She looked up slowly; her eyes seemed completely desolate.

"I don't know if I can do this," Gillian's voice seemed hollow.

"Gilly…" Candice walked up to her and caressed her hair. "I know that this is very hard for you, baby. You have to think of Catty," Candice reminded her.

Gillian then looked up and into Candice's eyes.

"More time with Catty, baby," Candice said sadly. "This baby will be happy in heaven, Gilly. No pain, all it will know is love."

Gillian stared at her as tears rolled down her face unchecked. Her body suddenly began to shake as she could no longer control the sobbing. "Why has God done this to me? Why, Candice?" Gillian tried getting up only to have her knees bend with her anguish. Candice suddenly was there holding her up as the cries were ripped from her soul. "Why my baby? Why my baby?"

Candice began to cry too as she held on tightly to Gillian. "I know, Gilly, I know."

At that moment the nurse and the doctor came in and helped her back up onto the gurney.

"No, no, I can't…" Gillian cried in desolation.

"Doctor?" Candice looked pleadingly towards the doctor.

"Gillian, your baby will never know pain, because that's all that it would feel if it were born," the doctor said to her as he leaned closer to her. "You don't want this baby to suffer. And bringing it into this world it would only know suffering. "

Gillian winced and seemed defeated suddenly. She wept silently as they took her to surgery. Candice walked beside her holding on to her hand tightly.

"Stay with me. Candy…please, don't let me go." Gillian sobbed suddenly.

"I will be right next to you. I won't let go. I won't let go I promise."

†

The next day came and went, and Gillian did not come. Adele was pacing the library like an angry cat. She had been irritable with everyone that she came into contact with that day. She could not control her reactions, her emotions, or the harshness within her that just spilled out. Being out of control had never been an issue for her. Emotions like anger, disgust, and desolation were coming at her from every side and she was not dealing with them as she thought she should. Adele had always felt very much in control of her life. Now, she had no control whatsoever over herself, and recognizing it only made things harder.

It was Catty's bedtime when the nanny brought her to Adele to say goodnight a few hours later.

"Contessa, Catty came to kiss her mama good night."

Adele opened her arms to her little girl and hugged her tightly to her as she closed her eyes, shutting out the fear that this too would be something she might be losing in the future.

"Where's Mommy?" Catty said as she pulled out of her mother's embrace slightly while she looked around the room.

"She's delayed, darling," Adele said as she kissed her daughter's forehead.

"I want Mommy," Catty began to pout.

"Now, now, my *principessa,* none of that," Adele said to her petulant child. "Nanny will read you a story and I will come tuck you in soon."

"When will my mommy come?" Catty would not let the subject go. She was as determined as her dark-haired mother if not more. Adele looked down at her daughter and a part of her admired the streak of strength she saw more and more in her daughter's character.

"Your mommy will be home soon, my darling. Now, bedtime for you." Adele handed the child over to the nanny and went back to her desk as they left the library.

Adele waited until the door closed to make her phone call.

†

"Hello?" Candice spoke wearily into the receiver.

"I want to speak to Gillian," Adele demanded.

"She is not here, Adele."

"Where is she!"

"Not here," Candice responded in irritation.

"If she doesn't call me within the next hour I am going to go and get her and not even God himself will be able to stop me. Now you tell her to call me!" Adele slammed the phone down in frustration and anger; she was seething with emotion she could no longer rein in.

Candice put the phone down and closed her eyes tightly. "My poor Gillian."

Candice walked to the nearest chair and sat down. She leaned her head back as her body began to shake with sobbing. Her mind filled with what had transpired a few days earlier. Gillian had gotten very pale as she squeezed Candice's hand tighter. At one moment she seemed like she

156

was about to speak before her eyes closed and tears rolled down the side of her face.

Candice heard an intake of Gillian's breath and at that moment she knew that it was over. She looked towards the doctor who nodded his head. Her attention went back to Gillian, her hand tightened, and she began to sob inconsolably. Somehow, she had known the very second that her child was taken from her.

"My baby, my baby is gone...oh God, my baby is gone!"

Candice began to weep as she held tightly to Gillian whose cries only seem to worsen. The nurse turned away with tear-filled eyes as the doctor began to finalize the procedure.

"God forgive me... please, God forgive me." Gillian cried hysterically.

Candice found no words as she continued to hold her and cry with her.

Candice could not stop the images of that moment from flooding her mind as she shut her eyes tightly again. They had to sedate Gillian in the end. And now she would also have to deal with Adele. Candice got up slowly and went into her bedroom. She had come home to take a shower and change. Gillian had had a terrible night and Candice needed to get back to her as soon as she could. The few times Gillian had woken she would not stop crying. The light that had always been in Gillian's eyes was suddenly gone and it broke Candice's heart to look at her.

†

Candice walked quietly into the private room of the clinic that Gillian was in. The procedure usually was a walk-out procedure but Gillian's reaction to it had been so upsetting that they decided to keep her overnight for observation. When Candice was walking down the hallway toward Gillian's room, she could not fail to notice the sad looks coming from the nurses on call that had witnessed the desperately sorrowful reaction of the beautiful young woman in the private room of the clinic. Gillian's mournful sobbing for her baby had touched all around her. Candice lowered her head and tried to muster up the strength to be strong in front of Gillian before she entered the room. Gillian was asleep when she walked in, and Candice sat down and waited for Gillian to wake up. She closed her eyes as she leaned her head back and she fell into a light sleep.

†

In the meantime, Adele kept calling the penthouse getting no answer. As the day progressed her anger knew no bounds. She was rude to Gloria and anyone that came into contact with her. Her hold on herself was progressively worsening and she was unable to stop herself.

"Edward, hurry up. The Contessa de Caravagio is on the line, and she doesn't sound happy," said the clerk from the front desk.

"Thanks, Jimmy, forward the call to my office," Edward said as he began to walk quickly towards his office.

"This is the fifth time she has called within the last two hours," Jimmy said nervously.

"Why didn't you page me, Jimmy?" Edward now sounded irate. "Never mind, let me take the call and then you and I have to talk."

Edward closed the door to his office behind him and quickly picked up the phone.

"Contessa..."

"Where is my wife?" Adele demanded.

"Contessa, Mrs. Visconti left the penthouse a few days ago and she has not returned," Edward answered quickly.

"And her friend?"

"Ms. Wentz was here today and left within the hour."

"I want to know as soon as Mrs. Visconti returns, do you understand?"

"Yes, Contessa." Edward visibly relaxed as he hung up the telephone. The Contessa was used to having her requests seen to quickly. She had bought the building seven years prior and now it was one of the most prestigious addresses in the Upper East Side. Her only request had always been to have the best; all else would fall into place and she had been right. The fact that she sounded angry was certainly not good. He knew that her being unable to reach him for the last two hours was totally unacceptable and undoubtedly it would have negative repercussions.

†

Candice slowly opened her eyes and found Gillian looking at her.

"Hi," she said softly as she got up and took Gillian's hand.

Gillian smiled a little as her eyes teared up.

"Would you like to talk to Catty, Gilly?" Candice asked hoping beyond hope that the thought of Catty would help Gillian.

"Yes, please, I…" Gillian was unable to say another word.

"Okay, honey, I'm going to call her right now, okay?"

Candice picked up the phone and made her call.

"I am calling for Mrs.….Mrs. Visconti would like to speak to her daughter, can you put her on the phone, please?"

Candice listened and handed the phone over to Gillian.

"Hello. Yes, Tomasina, it's me. Can you put my daughter on the phone for me?"

160

Gillian waited a few minutes and the visible change in her face became suddenly obvious as she smiled. "Hello, my sweet baby."

Candice sat down nearby, turning away slightly from Gillian. She wept as she heard Gillian talking to her little girl. Her chest tightened as she realized just how much she loved the women in front of her. Never in her wildest dreams did she ever imagine that she could possibly love Gillian more and at that moment she wished that she could give up her own life so that Gillian might know some happiness again. One day Gillian would be gone, and her world would be over. When this nightmare started, she had just wanted to spend as much time as possible with her. She never considered the consequences, nor did she care what they were.

When Gillian had left her life years before, she realized that nothing seemed as real, and her emotions had somehow become unnecessary to her. In other words, she had not felt much of anything. And now...now she knew that when Gillian died, she would die, too. She had simply not allowed herself to think that Gillian would die but now she couldn't imagine living without her and Gillian dying was all she ever thought about. Gillian was again in her life, and she suddenly realized that she had just existed all the years without her. Her love, her Gillian...she had always been so beautiful and so wonderful. Even now as the woman she loved seemed to fade more and more each and every day so did the world. Her light was going out and she did not want to live in the darkness that would follow her passing. That was Gillian; no wonder Adele was going crazy without her. It seemed an odd thing to think at that moment. Adele, the person who had taken what she most loved must be feeling the loss…the loss of Gillian as she too felt it now.

†

Adele walked in as Catty was replacing the telephone receiver.

"What is going on?" Adele asked angrily.

"Contessa…Mrs. Visconti wanted to speak to Catty," the maid said nervously in confusion.

"Mommy, I talk to Mommy," Catty said excitedly with a big smile on her face. "She is going to take me for ice cream."

"Of course, she is, my *principessa*. Go with Tomasina and tell nanny to take you to the pond to feed the ducks, okay?"

Catty giggled and Tomasina followed her out.

"Contessa…"

"It's all right; a mother has a right to speak to her child," Adele said distantly as she looked away sadly.

Tomasina quickly turned and went after Catty.

Adele sat down at the nearest chair to her and just stared in front of her. Where was Gillian?

Three hours later Edward called and informed her that Gillian was once again up in the penthouse.

The next morning Gloria let her know that she had spoken with Gillian earlier that morning and had been informed that she would meet them at the fundraiser. Adele said nothing; she simply walked out of the room and slammed the door behind her.

†

"I wish you wouldn't go," Candice argued again. "Gillian, you are just not strong enough yet."

"I need to do this. She's expecting me." Gillian continued to dress as she spoke to Candice. "Please help me."

"You don't have to do this!"

Gillian turned quickly and faced Candice. "Yes, I do. I need to, Candy."

Candice walked away after staring at her for a while.

Gillian sat down and closed her eyes. She knew that Candice was right. She wasn't strong enough yet, but she also knew that she had to. Perhaps that was the wrong way to put it. If she didn't go, Adele would be angry and might even come to confront her. The truth of the matter was she wanted to see Adele. She needed to see her. A part of her needed the solace that only Adele could give her. In her mind, the loss of her baby was Adele's loss too and, as such, she would be the only one that could possibly feel that emptiness as well. Gillian knew none of it made any sense, but she also knew that in this instance, the only one that could comfort her was Adele even if she didn't know what had happened, what she had done.

Candice loved her and she would try not to hurt her any more than she had already. She had reached out to her lifelong friend and had inadvertently touched and rekindled the love in Candice. In retrospect, she was sorry she had sought Candice's help. She had been selfish and now she was hurting her friend all over again.

She admitted to herself that she was being selfish too. She was only thinking of herself. She wanted to see Adele, to look at her, to breathe the same air with her, to touch her and from that get some comfort for the pain that now seemed to fill her whole being. Gillian opened her eyes and took a deep breath before she got up slowly. Adele, she needed to see Adele, or she would not be able to survive another moment.

† 

Gillian's cab pulled up in front of St. Anthony's where the fundraiser was to take place. She stepped out of the cab and found Gloria, one of Adele's many assistants, suddenly next to her.

"Hello, Mrs. Visconti, the Contessa instructed me to wait for you and lead you to the reception area. She arrived about thirty minutes ago."

"Thank you, Gloria." Gillian smiled a little.

"Are you all right?" Gloria asked as Gillian seemed to lean towards her.

"Yes, I'm fine. Thank you, Gloria." Gillian tried to reassure her. "Let's go to the Contessa, she doesn't like to wait."

"Right this way, Mrs. Visconti." Gloria led the way.

It seemed that people just stopped talking as Gillian walked in. She looked ethereal in her beauty. Her hair was piled up and exposed her elegant neck and shoulders. The colour of the light blue of her dress highlighted her eyes all the more. Adele turned and could not hide the love that seeing Gillian brought itself to her features.

Adele walked over to her and noticed the delicacy of the woman in front of her. So beautiful, Gillian had always seemed so beautiful, but tonight there was something in her features that made Adele just want to hold her and caress her. Instead, when she was in front of Gillian, her eyes searched the eyes now in front of her and suddenly she experienced a sadness that seemed to tear at her very soul. To hide her embarrassment, she simply leaned down and kissed Gillian lightly on the mouth for all to see.

"Hello, darling, we have all been waiting for you." Adele turned towards the group closest to her and started making the introductions. She did not look towards Gillian again until much later. Every time she met Gillian's eyes something inside her hurt more than she could bear. It wasn't something that she could point to, but Gillian moved and spoke as if from a distant place and this resonated somehow within Adele. All she understood was that she craved the closeness at the moment in a way she could not understand, so she walked towards Gillian and walked her to their table with her hand possessively touching her back. At the merest touch Adele felt she was able to breathe.

The dinner went as expected. Speeches were given and the sponsors were thanked accordingly. In the end, they asked Gillian to stand up to recognize the generous donation that, through her interest and efforts, the Caravagio Foundation had given to the organization.

The dinner progressed to music and usually this was when Adele and Gillian would make their excuses and head home. But tonight, Adele seemed uninterested in ending the evening. She continued the conversation with some of the board members seated at the table with them. Gillian seemed happy to listen but had begun feeling the strain that her body was beginning to fail her. She raised her hand to her temple and closed her eyes for a moment. As her hand came back down to the table it landed softly over Adele's which immediately brought Adele's attention to her.

Adele's stare seemed to pierce right through her. The music suddenly softened, and Adele got up and put her hand out to her. Gillian placed her hand in it and followed her to the dance floor without a word spoken from either of them.

All gazes seemed to go towards them as they walked to the dance floor hand in hand. It was common knowledge that they were a couple but to see them in an intimate embrace made curiosity come alive. Adele and Gillian had never given such demonstrations as they were doing tonight by openly dancing in front of all. They were so engrossed in each other that they just didn't seem to care who saw them. There were a few photographers that were clicking away. Tomorrow the photos would without a doubt be on a few front pages. The spectators could only look as their bodies seemed to become one and no one could argue the beauty and the love shared by the two women now on the dance floor.

As soon as Adele had stepped onto the dance floor and had faced Gillian, her arms were filled with the softness of her. Gillian melted into her, and Adele's eyes closed with an emotion she could not control. Her arms went around Gillian's body and pulled her closer still. Gillian's perfume filled her senses, her lips sensually caressed Gillian's ear as her hands caressed her back. She was so desperate and hungry for her but tonight had seemed all the more important to have Gillian in her arms.

Gillian had not fought the need to be held. She needed the comfort of Adele's embrace; she needed the closeness of her body. Her hands went up over Adele's neck and allowed the embrace to deepen. The music filled the air and touched the emotions that they had once shared, causing Gillian to feel the desperation of connecting that was getting harder and harder to control.

Adele seemed to sense something and pulled her closer still. Gillian sought the security of the embrace she needed and told herself that for this one moment she needed Adele more than life itself. She buried her face in her lover's neck and her lips kissed the skin that enticed them. For one moment she had dared to dream. As she slowly realized the enormity of her action her eyes filled with tears, and she pulled away.

Adele did not try to hold her and followed her back to their table. Confusion reigned inside Adele. Gillian had kissed her. It had been Gillian's lips that had lightly kissed her neck. Adele followed her in a daze unable to process or understand what was happening.

When Gillian reached the table, she turned towards Adele whose eyes were searching hers. Then all she knew was that she was in Adele's arms as the world suddenly began to spin and got dark.

"Someone help me!" Adele yelled as she was trying to hold onto Gillian as they began to fall to the floor.

Immediately they were surrounded by some of the doctors present at the benefit. Gillian was rushed to the emergency room with Adele beside her. Adele held her hand

and kissed it many times as she whispered words of love to her.

All that mattered at that moment was that something was wrong. She felt deeply that something was very wrong. And not understanding why, in her desperation, her love went out to Gillian with no reservations.

Gillian opened her eyes slightly and Adele kissed her lips and caressed her face. Gillian seemed to come in and out of consciousness. Once or twice, she whispered "Dell…" and the sadness in her voice cut deeply into Adele's heart as she saw tears running out of Gillian's eyes.

The emergency room doctor came in to speak to her. She turned to look at him but never released Gillian's hand.

"What's happened? What is wrong with my wife?"

"She is hemorrhaging. Right now, we have to stop that. We are not sure what caused it yet." The doctor answered cautiously.

At that moment Dr. de Lanpandusa walked in followed by Margot not far behind him.

"I will see to everything, Contessa. May I see the chart, doctor? I am the Contessa's family physician."

"Of course, come this way, doctor." Dr. de Lanpandusa followed the emergency room doctor out.

Margot stayed and saw and listened as Adele again focused her attention on Gillian.

"*Amore mio*…open your eyes. *Per favore, cara mia,*" Adele's voice was filled with her anguish and concern.

"Dell…" Gillian again opened her eyes slightly and Adele's lips kissed her lightly over and over again.

"*Ti amo, cara mia. Ti amo.*" Adele then took her in her arms and caressed her hair as she kissed her cheek.

Margot walked out of the room and found herself face to face with Dr. de Lanpandusa.

"You have to do something. If this continues, she will tell her." Margot growled at him unable to control the anger rising in her.

"I never planned on this. But I know what will end this. I'll be right back." He walked away leaving her stunned.

Margot then walked back into the room. Gillian had obviously passed out again.

"Adele, darling, sit down, give her some room to breathe." Margot could not control the edge in her voice.

Adele stared back at her. "Wait outside, Margot."

Margot acted insulted and walked out of the room in a huff.

A few minutes later the doctor came back in and gave Gillian an adrenaline shot which seemed to revive her a little. Adele waited patiently on the other side of the bed still holding Gillian's hand.

The shot seemed to take effect a few minutes later as Gillian began to come back to consciousness.

"Gillian, can you see me?" The doctor asked.

"Yes," Gillian answered groggily.

"Let your eyes follow my finger."

Gillian's eyes did as instructed until her eyes met Adele's and they did not move away.

"I have been so worried," Adele said, filled with emotion as her eyes filled with unshed tears.

"Don't cry, darling..." Gillian said not realizing how the endearment had just slipped out. "I'm fine. You don't have to worry," she reassured Adele again.

Adele bent her head down and kissed Gillian's hand holding it against her lips as her eyes sought out Gillian's.

"Dell..." Gillian's hand caressed Adele's cheek softly.

At that moment Candice walked in and Margot smiled from the corner of the room.

"Gillian, are you alright?" Candice immediately went to Gillian's side and Gillian released Adele's hand.

"I'm just fine." Gillian now looked only towards Candice. In her weakness she had sought comfort from Adele and things would only be worsening now. At that moment she resolved to go forward. She had killed her baby and now she must be cruel to save Adele. No matter how much it cost her, she would save Adele.

"What happened?" Candice asked concerned.

"I fainted. I will be fine, honestly," she reassured Candice.

Candice stared at her realizing that there was only so much she could say in front of Adele. She leaned down to kiss Gillian on the cheek and Gillian turned her face and kissed her fully on the lips. "I'm alright, darling," Gillian said looking into Candice's eyes.

Adele stared unable to move as Gillian's lips kissed Candice once more. A moment ago, Gillian had called her darling. Adele's world began to spin and fall off its axis. She then simply walked out of the room and out of the hospital. She walked faster and faster, looking for air to fill her lungs. She reached the outside and took bursts of air to fill her lungs with life. Life…what life? Her mind and her heart were at odds and confusion filled her with such a fog that she could not find herself to get out. She got into the car waiting for her and never looked back.

†

After walking out of the hospital that night something just shut down in Adele. Seeing Gillian kiss Candice had been the ultimate betrayal to her. That one kiss had made it crystal clear to her that she had never truly known Gillian. For a moment that night, she had believed that they were still in love, that there had been a mistake somehow, a misunderstanding, and that they would be together again. That one kiss had shown Adele just how much of a deceiver Gillian could be. She felt used and she was angry. Gillian had fooled her, used her, and had made her love her and it all made Adele angrier and angrier. Gillian would never make a fool of her again no matter what it cost her.

Things between them after that night were civil at best. Seething anger mixed with undying desire made for an explosive powder keg that time eventually would not be able to control. When it was her turn to have Catty, Gillian would come and stay occasionally. The times that Gillian did not come, Adele never inquired why anymore. They regularly attended public functions, but rarely spoke to one another. Adele did not even try to be civil. Her veneer was beginning to crack even in public.

Carlo began to visit Gillian at the penthouse regularly once or twice a week when he was home. He and Adele argued over it, but she did not stop him from continuing. Gradually, Adele began to realize that she was slowly losing all that she once thought was hers forever. Gillian had promised to love her forever; Adele, who believed in nothing, trusted no one, had believed the words. The betrayal was becoming more than she could bear on a daily basis and something inside her began to fester.

Catty began to adjust to the new family schedule and didn't complain as much about not having her other mommy always present. They were all adjusting to the changes in their lives. Adele however was becoming progressively more sombre and detached from all around her. The cold inside her was taking over her world and this time she knew she would not survive it. A part of her welcomed the oblivion that began to fill her; the other part of her was still so filled with love that it choked her with its pain as a tidal wave of something wild began to take birth.

One afternoon Margot walked into the library and found her looking out the window as she usually did when Gillian would come to drop off Catty.

"Will she be staying this time?" Margot asked angrily.

"I don't know," answered Adele without turning to face her sister.

"How much longer are you going to behave this way?"

Adele turned towards her aggressively "What way?"

"Like a love-sick puppy staring out that window!" Margot blurted out. "Look at yourself, you're a wreck."

"This is not your concern." Adele suddenly stood straighter in all her arrogance.

"You are my concern. I love you, Dell," Margot said as she approached her.

"Don't you ever call me that!" Adele said seething as if something had erupted in her.

"Why? Because that whore calls you that. She doesn't love you! She's with another woman. When is that going to sink into your head?" Margot spat at her.

At that moment Adele was unable to control her fury and slapped Margot hard across the face.

Margot stared at her in disbelief as Adele shook from the anger within her. "Have you lost your mind?" Margot stood holding her cheek.

"Don't you ever address my wife in that fashion!"

"Your wife?" Margot said mockingly.

"That is what she is. Never forget that, Margot. Never ever forget that again. Even she recognizes that."

"You are carrying this too far, aren't you, darling?" Margot said sarcastically.

"No, I'm not. I married her before God, Margot," Adele stated.

"You what?" Margot could not believe that Adele had gone that far. "You did not marry Carlo's father in a church intentionally; that was a point in the past that you had always stood by. You said that marriage was a sham, you don't believe in God, you made that clear constantly to me, Adele...what are you talking about?"

"I wanted her to be mine in every way. I wanted to believe in all of it." Adele suddenly seemed tired. "She is in here." Adele's fingers pointed to her chest. "I told her I loved her and that I would be true to her till my dying breath. She said I was her love...she promised to never walk away." Adele's eyes filled with unshed tears. "That made her mine. That made her my wife inside me. I have to believe that there is still a part of me in her. That thought, and that thought alone, keeps me from losing my mind." Adele took a deep breath, and her demeanour began to pale. "Look at her ring finger, Margot. My ring is on it still. She may say that she is not mine, but I once held her heart, I held her body, she gave me her soul and I loved her. I love her even now when she lives with Candice. No matter what happens, inside me she will always be mine. I can't tear her out of me. Even now when she denies me, even now as I am filled with nightmares of her in Candice's arms… Even now I love her. I gave her all of me, I can't deny that. I fight it but, I can't deny it."

"You are playing the fool in this ridiculous farce. Don't you see that? She is making a fool of you!"

"Stay out of it. This is not your concern." Adele suddenly sounded weary, closed her eyes for a second and breathed in deeply as if to steady herself. She turned and went to the window as she heard the noise of an approaching vehicle.

Adele left the room as she saw the car approaching the front of the house. Margot walked towards the window as the car pulled up and Gillian got out of the vehicle. Catty then followed and ran into the waiting arms of Adele as she stepped out of the house.

Margot touched her cheek. "We'll see how long you think of her as your wife. You never truly loved the others. You should never have fallen in love with her. They all lie. I'm going to teach you they all lie. One day you are going to thank me for it."

# CHAPTER NINE

Adele looked for Gillian's ring finger. Gillian no longer wore the ring. Adele remembered buying it with so much love, something of hers that would touch her lover. For a moment, she thought she saw something, but she knew better. Gillian, like her words, only held lies. Adele's body stiffened as her soul pulled away. She had but a minute ago reaffirmed her love for Gillian in front of Margot, and now all she felt was the pain that loving gave her. Her heart hardened as her soul began to die once more. What little hope remained in her died a bit more each and every day. She fought reality but the frozen cold of it was taking over her very being.

Adele turned to her daughter and gave Catty her undivided attention. "Come, little one, mama has a surprise for you," Adele said excitedly as she picked up Catty and walked into the house with her daughter in her arms. Gillian followed them in silently. Gillian never noticed the crease between Adele's brows as she held back a sob that reached her very soul. Pain, it seemed, had become a constant inside them.

"Gillian!" Carlo said excitedly as he ran down the steps when he saw Gillian enter the foyer.

"Carlo, hello sweetheart." Gillian wrapped her arms around him and kissed him on the cheek as he rushed into her embrace. "How did you do against your archenemies?"

Adele listened in fascination as she tried desperately to control the turmoil inside her.

"We won by two points." Carlo laughed heartily as he released her from the bear hug. "It was close. Are you coming to the next one?"

"Of course, nothing could keep me away," Gillian said as she hugged him again. "You were great you know."

"Thanks," Carlo said as he blushed.

"My surprise, Mama, my surprise," Catty insisted in her mother's arms.

Carlo and Gillian turned to them. Adele then looked down at her daughter and smiled. "*Vieni piccola.*"

They followed her to the courtyard behind the house. Catty began to clap her hands excitedly when she saw the pony. Adele smiled at the delight expressed by her daughter. At least she got this right. She was able to make her little girl happy.

Gillian's mouth opened in surprise, then her displeasure showed in her face.

"Come, my *principessa*, let's meet your pony." Adele carried her daughter towards the pony.

Gillian was filled with fear. All she could see was Catty being hurt as she fell off the pony. How could Adele have done this without discussing it with her first? Carlo looked from his mother to Gillian and knew that an argument would be following very soon.

As Adele was about to place Catty on the saddle Gillian spoke up. "Please don't."

Adele turned to her in confusion and exasperation, "Why not? I got her the pony so that she could ride it."

"We need to talk about this, Dell," Gillian insisted.

"Mama, pony please." Catty pouted as she tried to get out of Adele's arms, trying to grab the pony.

Adele challenged Gillian's stare. This was her time with her daughter and Gillian was not allowed to interfere in that, not anymore.

"Catty, why don't we walk the pony so that she gets to know you, okay?" Carlo took his sister from his mother's arms and he and Catty walked away happily leading the pony by the reins.

"Why would you do something like this without discussing it with me first?" Gillian approached her in anger and disbelief.

"I don't need your permission to give my daughter a gift," Adele replied angrily. "Your opinion is not necessary to me. I don't need your permission for anything I want to do, Gillian."

"You do when it comes to our child. She is too young for a pony, Dell," Gillian said as she got closer to Adele.

"She is almost three; I was two years old when I rode my first pony."

"And that's how you got that scar near your left temple," Gillian replied.

Adele touched her left temple and remembered when she had told Gillian about the scar. It had been one night in the beginning after when they had made love. Gillian had kissed her scar many times over. Adele looked at Gillian and as she did, she knew that Gillian had remembered, too.

"I don't want our baby to get hurt, Dell. She's still too fragile. Let's wait just a little longer." Gillian was asking in her usual soft way. She had always known how to talk to Adele. Even now she had a hard time refusing Gillian.

"Catty is stronger than I ever was," Adele said introspectively as she looked towards the children walking the pony.

"Catty is so like you," Gillian said softly, and Adele looked towards her again. "She's so like you, Dell. I just…I couldn't bear it if anything happened to her," Gillian finished saying as her eyes filled with tears.

"I would never let anything happen to her. I will be with her every moment she is on the pony," Adele insisted.

The tears spilled out of Gillian's eyes. "It's always your way." Gillian walked back inside without saying another word.

Adele stared at her as she walked back into the house. Had that been an issue between them? Had she always had to have things her way? Her memories were uncertain and could not be trusted these days. Nothing that she believed to be true once was real anymore. Gillian was with Candice, and that was a reality that she had to come to terms with. Gillian had never loved her. All the words had been lies, all the promises of love had been empty words. Adele closed her eyes and breathed deeply trying to control the emotions within her.

Carlo brought Catty back to her when he saw Gillian go into the house. He waited in silence to see what his mother would do.

"Mama, pony please."

"It's yours, my *principessa*. When you are bigger you can ride him. What will you call him?" Adele tried to appease the child.

Carlo smiled to himself, but then he wondered again why was this happening? Surely, he wasn't the only one that saw that Gillian and his mother still loved each other. He just didn't understand, and they refused to address it with him. At first, he had thought that it had something to do with the woman that lived with Gillian at the penthouse. But he could tell right away that the relationship they had was nothing like the one that Gillian had always shared with his mother. Gillian cared for Candice, he could tell, but the look in her eyes when she saw Adele was undeniable. He saw it in the way his mother and Gillian spoke to each other; it wasn't what they said it was how they looked at one another; that was something that neither could hide. It was also the way their voices softened. It was in the distant looks of hidden loneliness. They always seemed to want to say more. He would try to talk to his mother again soon.

†

Gillian was looking at them from a window close by as she saw Adele walk the pony with their daughter by the hand. A part of her was happy that there was still something in Adele that she was able to reach. The last two months had been horrible between them. Adele had cut her off emotionally. It had been what she had wanted, but she had not counted on just how hard that would feel. The last time she had not stayed at the house. It was more than she could handle, feeling the coldness with which Adele treated her. This time she was staying because she needed to see her lover even if she knew that it would hurt. She kept telling herself that she was doing the right thing. This was best for both of them, and yet the right thing felt so wrong. She closed her eyes and dreamed. Dreaming of her love was all that she had to get her through her day lately.

Later that night she looked on as Adele put their daughter to bed. How she missed the everyday things like this with Adele. Carlo running down the stairs, and having dinner together, as they had done tonight as a family. She had felt the distance from Adele but a part of her remembered how it had once been, and that memory, that longing for the past, was like a drug that she had begun to need and couldn't do without. She remembered in the past how, when they sat down to dinner, the happy chattering between them and the children never seemed to end. They planned their garden and the colour schemes of the renovations to the house. Everywhere she looked there were memories that had been created of their lives together. It had all been so perfect. They had been so happy. Memories of these times were sometimes more painful than her virus. The virus that weighed heavier and heavier each passing day.

Gillian felt pain most of the time now. The pills were no longer helping, and she had begun to experience more fainting spells. She no longer went out alone with Catty. She feared that she might faint, and Catty might be left defenseless. She felt her mortality more than ever on a daily basis. Her days were getting shorter and as she looked around the table during dinner, she let herself imagine how it once was again. She closed her eyes as she saw Adele kiss their little girl and say goodnight, and wallowed in the joy of it. There would not be many days like this left to her; she knew that they were getting shorter and shorter.

Adele had walked past her without saying a word.

# CHAPTER TEN

Gillian could not sleep. It seemed that she never slept much anymore. The new medication seemed to help her pain but would keep her from sleeping. She ran her fingers through her hair as she walked out of her bedroom. Perhaps a walk in the garden would help. She missed walking the garden at night. She and Adele had taken long walks when she was pregnant with Catty and was unable to sleep. How sweet and distant those times seemed now.

Gillian was coming down the staircase when her attention went towards voices coming from the opened door of the library. She took a few more steps down and stopped as soon as she saw Adele in her robe handing a young woman money.

"Please call me again," the woman said as she smiled and kissed Adele on the cheek.

"Paolo will drive you," Adele spoke softly.

The transaction that had taken place before her almost made Gillian double over with the pain, leaving her unable to move or breathe. She felt her knees give out as she unceremoniously fell onto the step, one hand on the banister, the other covering her mouth. The horror of what she had witnessed filled her whole being.

†

Adele stood by the door and watched the young woman as she walked away. As she turned back toward the library, she caught sight of Gillian on the staircase. Gillian stared back at her in accusation. Gillian turned suddenly and ran up the stairs with all the strength she had left in her. Adele ran after her. Both women filled with confusion and desperation ran for different reasons. Adele pushed her way into Gillian's bedroom as Gillian tried to shut the door.

"Get out!" Gillian cried out. "Get out!" She could not control the sobbing that wracked her body.

Adele pushed her way inside, grabbed Gillian, and pulled her hard against her. "Did you think that you were the only one allowed to fuck someone, *cara*?"

"Let me go! Let go of me!" Gillian cried all the harder as she pushed Adele away.

"You fuck Candice. Do you fuck her every night that you are not here?" Adele pulled her harder against her as Gillian fought to set herself free. Adele began to press her body harder against her and brought her leg between Gillian's. A guttural groan escaped her lips as she pressed harder against Gillian's center. Skin burned on skin and Adele was suddenly consumed with lust. Robes had opened and skin fused with skin. Adele's mouth went to Gillian's neck, and she began to suck with a hunger she had never known. Her body moved against Gillian, and she began to feel Gillian's wetness on her skin. Her head lifted and fell back in joyous abandonment. A groan escaped her as her mouth then hungrily took Gillian's lips.

†

Gillian's body reacted to her lover's touch. Sweetness, such desire and sweetness filled her that for one moment all she allowed herself to do was feel and wallow in the passion of her lover before her. When she felt Adele's hands begin to remove her robe and caress the side of her breast, Gillian began to struggle. She had to stop this...she had to. Suddenly desire had taken a different context. Adele's touch began to roughen as Gillian began to try and push her away. Her hand went down between Gillian's legs and her fingers felt the wetness she needed to taste again or die.

"No!" Gillian exclaimed in desperation.

"You're mine!" Adele growled as her grip tightened on Gillian's wrist and she began to kiss her again harder this time.

"Don't, please don't!" Gillian slapped her hard across the face.

Adele suddenly pushed herself hard away and Gillian landed on the bed, half recumbent. She could not look away from Adele as she wept. "Get out, please get out."

†

Adele stared at her, trying to understand. The blow to her face had stunned her. At that moment she felt the weight of the world on her shoulders. She closed her eyes and when she opened them again the sadness that now resided inside her was visible in them.

"I can't make love to a woman anymore, *cara*." Adele said wearily. Gillian suddenly looked at her in shocked silence and stared at Adele as tears still ran down her face. "I can't bear for anyone to touch me. I don't understand…why does it matter to you, when you don't want me?"

"Dell…" Gillian cried and covered her mouth as a sob escaped her and tears that she could not stop rolled down her face.

"I sent her away, Gillian. I couldn't touch her or bear it as she tried to touch me. I am dead inside. You have ruined me, I don't feel. I don't feel... all my body knows is you. And you don't want me... Why does it matter to you if anyone else touches me if you don't want me?" Adele could no longer hide her despair. Gillian saw it in her lover's eyes what she had never wanted to see. She had broken Adele's heart. She had broken Adele...Adele was broken.

Adele turned to leave the room and stopped with her back to Gillian as she was about to walk out the door. "I'm going away... I can't stay here any longer..."

Gillian sobbed. "Dell..."

"I won't take Catty. She belongs with you. Both children will be happier with you." Adele walked out and closed the door behind her.

†

"Dell..." Gillian lay her face down on the pillow and cried like she had done when she was a child. She would never see Dell again. This had been their final good-bye and it broke her heart to know that it had happened this way. She had gotten her way. She had done what she thought was right. What she had never counted on was the pain that her choice had brought to them. She was dying but so was Dell.

†

"This is not working. You promised that it would all be over by now!" Margot whined.

"*Cara mia*, it will happen," the male voice cajoled her.

"I am going back to Europe."

"No! You said you were going to stay here for good." The desperation came through in his voice. "Give me just a little more time, *cara mia*. Will you do that?"

"I won't wait forever. I want to believe you. I love being with you. Will I see you tonight?" she asked coyly.

"Yes, tonight at the same place."

†

"Hi, how was your weekend?" Candice asked as soon as she walked into the kitchen where Gillian was making dinner.

"It was fine." Gillian avoided looking at her as she spoke.

"Everything okay?" Candice waited. "Did Catty come back with you?"

"I left her with Dell. She wanted to take her to the zoo. I will pick her up tomorrow morning."

Candice looked at her as she saw the uneasiness grow in Gillian by the second.

"How was work?" Gillian asked as she continued to stir the contents of the pot.

"I am fitting in nicely. Selsnik visited our offices back in Wisconsin about a year ago."

"He is the senior partner, right?" Gillian briefly looked at her and smiled slightly.

"Yeah."

"I'm glad that this is working for you, Candy." Gillian smiled and began to stare at the pot again.

"So, how was it really?" Candice asked. She began to rub Gillian's back as she held her in a light embrace.

Gillian looked up and faced Candice. "She's going away."

"Catty…"

"She's not taking Catty. She's leaving both children with me." Gillian began to cry as she went into Candice's arms. "I don't know if what I'm doing to her is worse than just telling her the truth."

"Oh honey…" Candice stroked her back as she held her tightly. Gillian seemed to be getting smaller and smaller. She had begun to feel her ribs more. As much as Gillian tried to hide the weight loss, it was beginning to be more and more visible.

Gillian pulled away slowly and walked a few steps away with her back to Candice.

"I'm going to tell her. I thought I was doing the right thing. I wanted to protect her. And…I don't think anyone has hurt her as much as I have. Maybe I am being selfish to want her till the last minute of my life." Gillian began to sob as she wrapped her arms around herself. "I need her, Candice. I need her so much…"

Candice was immediately next to her holding her tightly. She held Gillian to her not exactly sure if she could stand the ramifications of those words now.

"Take a few days to think it over, honey. If that is what you want to do, then do it. But give yourself some time to think about what this will mean, okay?"

Gillian nodded in Candice's embrace.

Candice held Gillian to her possessively. Gillian would never go back to Adele. Gillian had been hers first. She had the right; Gillian was where she belonged. Moving to New York had been taking a big chance but she would use all her influence to keep Gillian. She told herself over and over again that she knew Gillian. She knew what was good for her. And Gillian would eventually come to agree with her. It was just a matter of time; time…time was the one thing they didn't have. All the time that Gillian had left would be hers.

When Gillian went to pick up Catty the next day, she was informed that Adele had gone to a board meeting. Gillian took this as a sign that she should indeed give more thought to her decision to tell Dell or not.

# CHAPTER ELEVEN

---

"Contessa, we haven't seen you in the office in quite some time." Georgio Passeti, her VP of Acquisitions in the New York office, welcomed her as she walked in.

"Hello, Georgio, I may not be here often but, I know all that goes on here," she said with a sardonic smile.

"You, Contessa, are a remarkable woman. Anyone that doubts that is a fool. Please sit." He smiled in agreement and pointed to the chair in front of him. "What has brought you here?"

"There are some things that I am wrapping up here for the next few days and I came to bring you up to date."

"I will clear my calendar."

Adele began tying up all loose ends in New York. She included Georgio in all the meetings since he would be overseeing all of the projects in New York for at least the next year. Adele was going back to Europe to focus on the winery. She had extensive plans for its growth and some of the preliminaries were also being arranged from New York.

That particular morning was as busy as the others had been when she was interrupted by her personal secretary.

"Contessa, I have Sabina from billing here and she wishes to speak to you personally."

Adele thought for a moment and asked Diane to show Sabina in.

Sabina had been working for Adele for over ten years. She had rendered Adele a few considerations from time to time in the past. Usually bills of questionable references that should not be put through the office to avoid embarrassment or speculation of her past indiscretions. The press had people everywhere and some things were better dealt with privately than put through the company and made real by existing paperwork. Sabina had been a loyal employee, and because of that, she was held in high regard by Adele.

"Come in, Sabina." Adele stood up. "Sit down please." Adele looked towards Diane that was lingering at the door. "You may leave us, Diane."

Diane closed the door behind her, and Adele sat back down and gave Sabina all of her undivided attention.

194

"You needed to speak to me?"

"Yes, Contessa." Sabina hesitated and seemed suddenly very uncomfortable in her chair.

"Sabina?"

"I...a bill came through, Contessa and..." she stuttered.

"Still? It's been years..." Adele trailed off in confusion.

"It's different." Sabina seemed more embarrassed by the second.

"Sabina, I can't imagine... I haven't..."

"It's not you, Contessa..."

"What? Please, Sabina tell me what this is all about." Adele could not figure out what it was. Sabina had brought her bills for dubious situations and they had been privately paid. Adele did not understand since she had not had any questionable incidents to cover up since she and Gillian had gotten together.

"This bill is for Mrs. Visconti. I wasn't sure how...I mean, I didn't know if you wanted it processed...or just taken care of privately." Sabina would not look at her in the eye as she handed Adele a piece of paper.

Adele took the paper from her and began to read it. Her features suddenly turned ashen as her hand began to shake.

"Contessa?" Sabina suddenly realized that she had delivered news that had shocked and surprised.

"Thank you, Sabina, you may go now." Adele heard herself say but did not recognize her own voice. She felt an incredible coldness fill her being. Her face felt hot and the bile rose from her stomach into her mouth. "Take care of the bill privately, Sabina, and thank you." Adele left an open-mouthed Diane as she stormed out of her office.

"Contessa, will you need a car?"

Adele was beyond rational thought. All she felt was an incredible fire growing out of her and all it wanted to do was burn and destroy. She walked out of the building and got into a cab. Rage, she was consumed by rage. The crushed piece of paper was still in her hand. All she felt was ire. It filled her, seeping into every part of her. Gillian had killed their child. Their son.

She was lucid enough to call the estate to ready the limousine and to have two of her bodyguards and Catty's nanny ready to leave with her as she arrived. Her eyes burned and her head hurt, and it throbbed. She felt like something was tearing her to pieces from within. Her heart was shattered beyond repair. The fire that was taking over her body felt like an inferno of heat and anguish. The anger that had been festering had become a raging volcano that could no longer be controlled.

Less than an hour later the limousine seemed to fly through the city streets like a black bird splashing the wet and dark streets as it flew through the night, crashing against the dark waters that would lead it to its demise. Adele knew that after today she would no longer exist. She was dead inside. It had begun when she found out how Gillian had betrayed her. Her life ended the moment that she realized that the woman that she had loved so deeply had never existed.

Gillian had toyed with her from the very first. Everything had been a lie. All that was left of her was primal and expendable. She simply felt only the cold. Her eyes had never been more focused nor her mind more alert and yet she felt lifeless and disconnected from the world. The heat that had consumed her had now turned to fire and ice as both coexisted within her. The frozen tundra began to spread like a mantel over all of her senses. She felt nothing but a controlled sense of no return as the molten lava was ready to consume all in her path.

Adele knew that the car that she was in was moving very quickly. The numbness that now permeated her whole being was devoid of any emotion, of any sense of what was real. She stared lifelessly at the buildings that appeared like continuous blurs. As the car pulled up to her destination, suddenly like a gap in time, a rush of cold air hit her as the car door opened like an unstoppable avalanche. It hit her so quickly that she felt a grotesque thing inside her step out of the car instead of the woman that had existed in her body previously and, like an animal bent on killing, she rushed to her target. She was savage, jury, judge, and executioner. She tasted blood in her mouth and her body moved fluidly like that of a wild animal running towards the kill.

One thought kept repeating itself in her mind over and over again. "She killed my son…she killed my son." Gillian's betrayal had taken her beyond what her mind could endure. Gillian had made her believe in love, and then she had betrayed her, used her, taken her child, made her look ridiculous. She would soon be the laughingstock of those that had warned her that people like her should never trust anyone because money was ultimately the object. Gillian had proved that no one had truly loved her for herself and not for the things that her money could buy. Gillian had betrayed her with Candice, wanted to take her child from her, and now she had discovered the ultimate betrayal. Gillian had killed her son. It would have been a son and Gillian killed him. Gillian had broken what had never been broken before. Gillian shattered her heart beyond reconstruction.

Liar! Gillian was a liar. A liar that had torn out all her belief that love was real, that she deserved it, and then led her to an abysmal coldness that she had never known. Her heart was beyond broken, and now all she had was the cold and she ran to it. The cold turned her to ice. She would never truly feel again; she would breathe but would never truly know that she was alive.

Adele rushed through the receiving area like a whirlwind. The two men that were accompanying her followed closely behind, as well as the nanny. She bypassed the manager that came up to greet her and she tossed him like a rag doll out of her way like the insignificant thing that she felt he was in that moment. Because the only thing that Adele knew was that she had to find Gillian. The man fell onto a chair, indignant at this treatment and stared at the power that had just pushed him aside. One of the bodyguards stared him down and the manager simply remained in place, keeping the words to himself.

As she entered the elevator, her fury was palpable, and everyone could feel it in the air. The elevator barely contained the anger gaining ground inside her; the ire that filled her lungs and the fire that made her skin burn with rage was spilling over. Ice had become fire once more. Within seconds the doors of the elevator opened and within steps she was in front of the penthouse door. Her fist hit it with such force that the door itself shook as she continued to pound it.

"Gillian!" She kept yelling and still no answer from within a minute later. She stepped aside as one of the men kicked the door open with one swift kick.

As soon as the pieces of what remained of the door swung open, she could see Gillian rushing towards them in shocked surprise. Candice came through another door towards them and immediately walked towards Adele, obviously angry at the forced entry. Before Candice could speak Adele struck her so hard that she fell back against a side table and seemed unable to catch her breath as she lay on the floor.

Gillian stared in horror at the woman that was approaching her. Adele's stare caused her to take a step back and turn to run from her. Adele moved swiftly, grabbing Gillian by the hair and roughly turned her around to face her.

"Where is my daughter?" Adele growled as her other hand grabbed Gillian by the neck. "Go, find her!" She shouted towards one of the men. The nanny followed to look for the child as well.

"Adele..." before Gillian could finish Adele shoved her hard against the wall.

"I should kill you," she said, seething as she pressed against Gillian again. Gillian tried to run by her, and Adele grabbed her by the hair and pulled her hard against her once more "I want to kill you...liar," She spoke the words seething through her teeth barely audible.

"Dell..." Gillian was barely able to say as Adele struck her hard across the face with relish and placed her hand over her mouth as she pushed her against the door. "Be quiet, you are going to scare our baby," she whispered into Gillian's ear in a sarcastic growl as she pressed her body harder against Gillian's.

†

Gillian heard Catty calling out and Adele answered saying that she would be going to be with her soon. Gillian heard as they went out the apartment and she knew at that moment that she had lost her daughter. Her eyes turned to Adele in horror and in confusion.

At the same time Adele's crazed eyes turned to her.

"Gillian!" Candice cried out from the other room.

"Keep her there!" Adele screamed at the man outside as she pushed Gillian farther into the bedroom and slammed the door shut behind her.

"Dell..." Gillian began to say as Adele struck her hard across the face yet again.

"Don't speak...liar, everything was a lie!" Adele accused her with all the anger inside her. "I believed you! But you are a liar! I want to kill you!"

Gillian's tears ran freely down her cheeks. "No Dell..."

"I'm dead inside... I am disgusted by you!" Adele ranted as she paced side to side like a caged animal. "You are my wife and you lay with her... I want to claw at my skin to remove you from it." Adele held her head with both her hands in utter rage. "I am going to rip you out of my head and my body even if it kills me!"

"Dell..." Gillian sobbed miserably.

Adele seemed disoriented for a moment as she turned to look at Gillian and her fingers lightly touched Gillian's face. Adele then stared at her fingers as if mesmerized only to look up and stare straight in Gillian's eyes with something akin to madness. Adele's eyes were unreadable to her.

A stranger was looking at her. There was no recognition and Gillian watched in horror as Adele stared back at her hand. Adele's hand had blood smeared on it...she then looked up with a venomous smile akin to utter pleasure. She licked the blood with her tongue as she stared at Gillian. At that moment Gillian screamed, "No!"

As Gillian went to her to stop her, Adele pushed her away from her so hard that Gillian began to really feel fear. She tried to reach the woman that had once loved her but to no avail; she realized that Adele was now lost to her.

"I am going to treat you like the whore that you are. You killed my son!"

Gillian stared at her in horror. She knew...Adele knew...her son? It was a little boy...she had killed their little boy...she had killed their dream. Gillian's eyes filled with tears; she did not know that it had been a little boy, her little boy. She welcomed Adele's attack, her anger. She heard the tearing of her clothes before the horror of the last time that Adele would touch her body. The madness that followed would haunt them both to their death. It wasn't sex nor was it violence; they had gone beyond that, neither would survive it and time would show that neither did.

†

Adele walked out of the room an hour later. She seemed lifeless and did not look at Candice as she walked out of the penthouse. When she was honest with herself, she knew that it had never been about Candice, it was about Gillian. Gillian had made the promises; Gillian had been the one that broke them.

Love had been a word that others used. Love had been something that had never truly held her. She had given Gillian her whole being, her dreams, her secrets, her passion, and a heart that had learned to beat for only one name. Adele had loved her beyond the realm of the possible and when her world came crashing down, she could not escape it. It had crushed her because she never had built her defenses against it. She had loved Gillian so completely that the word betrayal had simply never entered her thoughts. The first revelation impaled her, and her shocked senses only registered that her life was oozing out the wound that would never heal. All that followed simply tore the wound bigger and bigger. She then remembered the impact of the words when she first heard them from Gillian. "I choose her, I don't love you…" She had never truly been whole after that. The silence encased her, and the void had begun to take her back into its darkness.

The bodyguard had kept Candice outside the room. Candice had sat on the sofa in what seemed like a lifetime holding her bruised body and, as they left the apartment, she got up slowly. Every step that she took towards Gillian's bedroom took forever. She was scared; something told her that it would be painful. Finally, as she got to the door, she couldn't hold the sob that escaped her lips as she saw what Adele had done. She didn't care how her own body hurt because a part of it thought that she deserved the pain. After all, she too had betrayed. She wanted Gillian and this was her way of getting her back and she knew that.

Candice wept as she slowly walked to where Gillian lay. Gillian seemed lifeless. She stared at the rumpled bed sheets and then allowed herself to look at Gillian's body. Gillian lay naked and unmoving. Her eyes were dull, and her face was smeared with blood. She was bruised and a childlike whimper escaped her lips as Candice lightly touched her. Suddenly Candice saw the tears spill over Gillian's eyes, and she breathed a sigh of relief; till that moment she had not had the courage to question whether Gillian had been alive or dead.

"Gillie…oh God, Gillie," Candice sobbed as she covered Gillian with a sheet. She kept trying to cover her and trying not to meet her eyes again. "Oh God, Gillie…"

Suddenly Candice felt her hair being caressed. She immediately looked up at Gillian. The tenderness of it made her cry all the harder. She put her head down on Gillian's chest as she wept. "Oh, my baby…I'm sorry…I couldn't stop her; I'm so sorry, my baby. Forgive me…oh God, forgive me." Candice cried so hard that her body shook, a part of her felt the guilt of it all, too.

†

Gillian caressed her hair softly. "Shhhh...shhhh." Gillian continued to console her. Nothing mattered; nothing else would ever matter. She had lost her daughter and now she knew that she had killed her little boy. It had been a boy. The realization of that news had killed yet another part of her. Oddly enough in the maelstrom of all that violence that she had shared with Adele only moments before their lives together had ended. The blood, all that Gillian could think of was the blood that now bound them and separated them. The blood would always exist between them.

†

Adele walked out of the building in a daze. Her footing was unsure, and she stumbled once or twice trying to keep a hold of her sanity. What had she done? Gillian deserved it! She was a whore that had used her. She was a liar that had made her love her. She had tried to take her money, her child. She had humiliated her and had killed her son! She kept justifying her actions. But if all that were true, why did she feel such disgust at herself? What had she done? The horror of what had just occurred kept pushing itself into her head. She was a monster, but this was something that Gillian was to blame for as well. But why did she keep hearing the words in her head? So many words...so very many.

Liar, Gillian was a liar. She had loved her, she kept telling herself and Gillian had used her. Adele kept repeating the same thing over and over again. She wanted to make the whole world hurt like she did. She couldn't stand the pain inside her at that moment. Adele wanted to forget, she wanted to hurt her, to tear the hunger for her out of her body and her soul and now the pain was worse. She couldn't understand why the pain was worse now.

Every step she took she knew would take her farther and farther from the viper that she had loved. Because, even now, Adele knew that she would love Gillian to her dying breath. Death, she would welcome death. She felt like someone standing in front of a precipice. All she heard was a loud wind whirling around her body and inside her head. She heard nothing as she continued to walk as she kept reminding herself to breathe.

Adele looked dishevelled as she got into the limousine waiting for her in front of the building. All the occupants looked elsewhere except at her. Her daughter, held by the nanny, immediately went into her arms.

Catty caressed her mommy's face sweetly. "Mommy, you hurt yourself." Her little girl pulled her sleeve over her hand and began to wipe her mother's face. All the occupants watched as the child gently wiped away the blood smeared on her mother's face. Adele slightly turned her face towards her little girl and a sadness seemed to fill her as she looked at her child.

Adele's eyes suddenly filled with tears, and they began to run down her face unchecked and unnoticed by her.

"Don't cry, Mommy, I will kiss the boo boo away." Catty leaned in and kissed her mother on the cheek sweetly.

The tears however did not cease, and Adele finally looked into her child's eyes, pulled her to her gently and began to sob. "Oh God, oh my God, help me..." Her cries expressed the pain of her soul; she wept inconsolably as she held her child tighter to her. She caressed her little girl and rocked her back and forth sobbing. Why? Why? was the only word in her mind. Why? How could she do this? Why, when she had loved her? And the enormity of what she had just done created another wound within her soul. At that moment she wasn't sure who the monster was anymore.

Everyone in the car observing Adele could feel the sorrow and desperate sadness coming from her. Before them was a total opposite of the woman that had just committed such a heinous crime. The almighty Contessa suddenly seemed very human. She wept openly and for once in her life was not able to control what the world saw. They had all been in the service of the Contessa for many years. They had also, for the past few years, gotten to know Gillian. Their loyalty however, was never in question. The Contessa was who they owed their allegiance to. There was shock but not totally unexpected at what had happened. They had been in her employ long enough to know that the *"Aristos"* as they called people like her, were not bound by the same laws as them. Still, there were mixed emotions. They were appalled at what they suspected had happened behind that locked door, and yet they were overcome with empathy for the woman who so obviously was in such pain before them. The Contessa was human after all. Her tears and her pain were proof of that.

# CHAPTER TWELVE

Fall seemed to come early to New York that year, Candice thought to herself. It had been a few months since the day that changed everything. When she had walked into the bedroom and found Gillian she had been overwhelmed by the bruises and the bite marks on her body. Gillian seemed to give up on life since that day. They didn't talk about it. Gillian just faded away even after Dr. de Lanpandusa had assured her that the blood that Adele had been exposed to was not enough to infect her, a part of her just didn't believe him. Candice had mentioned Catty's name once and Gillian placed her finger on her lips. The pain she saw in Gillian was enough to make her never try to talk about it again.

She had tried to make Gillian talk about it. Candice's anger at Adele was fathomless. She had kept telling herself over and over again that Adele had to be punished. Gillian did address it once.

†

*"No more, let it go, Candice. Enough, no more pain…" Gillian's anguish in her voice made her want to stop talking about it but she could not stop herself any longer.*

*"She had no right to do what she did!"*

*"Neither did I."*

*"What? You are excusing her?"*

*"No, we both went too far," Gillian said sadly. "I knew what to do to push her away… I lied to her. To her I betrayed her, and still she wanted me. I then went further and further, to the point where I shattered something inside her that will never be whole again. I might have even given her a death sentence with this virus!"*

*Candice stared in disbelief.*

*Gillian then looked at her in tears. "I am the woman she loved who I betrayed with you. She gave me her heart to hold, and I broke it. She entrusted me with her secrets and a part of her that she never trusted to anyone. You think she hurt me? What she did to me killed her. It will torment her for the rest of her life. I did that, Candice!"*

*Candice remained silent then voiced all that she felt within her. "She's a monster."*

*"No Candy, to her I am the monster. I did that..." Gillian's body began to shake as she began to sob. "I should have told her the truth. It would have hurt her, but she might have survived it. I broke a beautiful heart, Candice. She gave it to me to take care of...she told me so and I broke it."*

*"Gilly, you are excusing her," Candice said softly.*

*"I killed her, Candice! Oh God, I killed her. She thinks I used her, that I didn't love her. I killed her. She found out about the abortion and that it was a little boy." Sobbing racked Gillian with pain.*

*Candice took Gillian into her arms. After that day, Gillian began to go further into herself. They never talked about it again.*

†

Candice walked out onto the balcony holding a tea tray, trying to put that memory away yet again. Her eyes searched for Gillian, and it hurt. The medicine didn't seem to help anymore. Gillian was huddled in a chair in the far corner of the balcony. Something inside her had just seemed to die, and memories of that day that she had just been thinking about filled her once more. Adele was not the only one that died that day, as Gillian had said. Candice now knew that Gillian had died, too. Candice looked up again and stared at

Gillian. She loved her; she had always loved her. And her eyes began to water as she looked at what remained of a once vibrant beautiful woman who now seemed always so peaceful of late that Candice was terrified every time she had to leave her alone. The fear that one day she would find that Gillian had left this earth made her heart ache. Adele was a monster. Nothing would ever make her change her mind about that. A monster that had destroyed a beautiful human being.

"Hello baby, aren't you cold out here honey?" Candice asked as she lay the tray down on the small table in front of Gillian and smiled at her.

"No, I'm fine. It's very nice out here." Her voice was calm and melodic and, as of late, lifeless.

Candice poured the tea for both of them, and, as usual, the time passed, and Gillian did not drink it. She just seemed to drift off onto a world of her own as she usually did these days. She was getting thinner and everyday her condition seemed to worsen. The pills she took didn't seem to help with the pain while she was awake. She slept too much as of late, too. She seemed to prefer oblivion instead of life.

The nightmares for Gillian were a constant as well. Every night she would wake screaming, completely drenched in perspiration. The woman Gillian loved was her demon and yet those were the arms that she wanted comfort from. Candice knew this as she watched in anguish and fascination.

Even now Gillian loved Adele. She would sometimes lay next to Gillian for hours thinking. The nightmares had become hers as well.

She should have done something. From the very first, Candice had acknowledged to herself that Gillian should be with Adele. She didn't want to know that, and she hated herself for even acknowledging it, but it was true. The guilt had begun slowly. She should have helped her, but Candice only thought of herself. She knew all along that it was wrong and now she shared the horror and the pain.

Candice had to look at herself at last and admit that she had wanted Gillian more than she wanted Gillian to be happy. Because she knew without a shadow of a doubt that Gillian would have found the peace she so desperately needed with Adele. Gillian loved Adele. And if Candice had truly loved her, she should have helped to make that happen. It was too late now. Candice wept. She admitted to herself that if Adele was a monster, then she was one too.

## CHAPTER THIRTEEN

---

People would just step out of the way rather than incur Adele's rage these days. Something inside her was always angry. There was a cruelness within her that was becoming entrenched in her very core. The gray began to appear in her temples like an outward extension of the icy coldness that had begun to take over her soul, and her eyes had become chips of cold steel. Where once upon a time she had enjoyed her takeovers or her business successes, they had now become a fix that she needed often to experience. Her plans for her beloved winery had become secondary in her life, although she was now running her empire from her estate in Italy. Her dream to take the winery to an international level had seemed to wane. Adele just simply didn't care. She had always been an astute businesswoman. She was now becoming known as a vicious one. Where in the past she had enjoyed taking over companies with dignity now the harder and the crueler it was the more she liked it. The deeper the dagger went into her opponent the more she enjoyed it. It had become a hunger that she never felt satiated from.

"Contessa, we don't need that. It's over and it's simply not necessary. It will take up time and cost money that we simply don't need wasted. Quite honestly, it's not worth the manpower that it will take, the company is ours." Giovanni, one of her new vice presidents in Italy, was explaining on the phone to her.

"Do it, I want to be there when you deliver the ultimatum, just do it," Adele growled with barely controlled anger. "We are not their friends. They should have just made it easy, and they chose a fight. Well, this is the spoils and I want them. So, set up the meeting and do it as I asked."

There was silence on the other end of the phone line for a mere moment then the words that she wanted were spoken. "Yes, Contessa, I will call you with the specifics."

"I want this wrapped up this week, Giovanni." She hung up, not waiting for a response.

There was a soft knock coming from the door. She looked up from where she was sitting. Her eyes were the outward reflection of the anger inside of her. She hated being interrupted when she was working.

Margot poked her head in. "Come, Adele, the children are ready."

"Margot, I don't have time..."

Margot let herself in and walked up to her sister. Her hand reached out lovingly and caressed her sister's hair. "The gray is spreading." Her hand then ran down her sister's face. Adele pulled away in annoyance.

"I don't have time." She turned away from Margot.

"Catty is fussy and is crying for her mommy." Margot waited for the response that she knew would follow.

Adele froze for a second, put her pen down, got up and walked out with Margot behind her to find and comfort her daughter.

†

Gillian leaned against the rail of the veranda. The world seemed so unreal. She closed her eyes and smiled at the breeze that caressed her face.

*"Close your eyes, tesoro mio,"* Adele whispered as *she was caressing her face with a rose.*

*"Mmmm, it smells heavenly." Gillian smiled with her eyes still closed.*

*"No, this is heaven, amore mio." Adele leaned in and kissed her lips with such sweetness that it had left her breathless.*

Gillian opened her eyes as a tear spilled and ran down her face. "Dell…"

Candice came out to the veranda and walked up to Gillian. She put a shawl over her shoulders. "It's getting cold out, I thought you might like this."

Gillian smiled at her then looked out over the city again and responded with barely a whisper. "Thank you."

†

Candice smiled but she knew that Gillian didn't even feel the cold anymore. Gillian had accepted death. She wasn't even fighting it anymore. Candice stood behind her and pulled her against her holding her tightly. She buried her face in Gillian's hair and closed her eyes. "I love you, Gillian."

†

In another part of the world, Adele was just as cold. She could not stop herself from thinking. *'And I am here surrounded in this darkness thinking of you, feeling you, wanting you still…after all this pain that always remains. I am filled with this music that never ceases to be and I feel you in every breath. Perhaps once I would have done anything to be with you, to want to make you want me but…I cannot stand this loneliness, but I cannot endure the thought*

*of seeing you again even more and that is my agony and why
I despair in this wanting tonight.'*

And again, the wine was drunk, and oblivion was
welcomed. The night was filled with nightmares and pain
and regret…so many regrets.

†

The morning comes and Adele wakes as she does
most mornings, alone, with a frightful headache and feeling
empty.

†

Catty had been fussy all day. And to Margot's
surprise, Adele's patience with the child was endless. Adele
was not the same, but she didn't care. Margot had finally
gotten what she wanted. Adele was back in Italy and this
time she would make sure that nothing would get in the way
of her plans.

Their mother was due to arrive soon, and her
presence would help as well. Adele hated Gillian, or at least
never mentioned her nor did she want to know anything that
had to do with her any longer. Gillian was simply a subject
that was not open for discussion with Adele. Margot was
happy Adele gave in to her insistence at times to have lunch
or take her to the opera or to some fashion show that Margot

wanted to attend. Then there were the times that Adele simply was oblivious to, the times that they shared, and that Margot planned for to the last detail. Tonight, she would fill her want yet again with Adele's body. Adele welcomed the first glass of wine with the drops added by her and the rest of the wine to follow simply just added to her plan.

†

Dusk, Adele hated dusk. She was leaning against the veranda watching the sun's farewell to the day when Margot joined her and handed her a glass of wine. She was glad to have some kind of relationship with her half-sister. She had loved Margot when she was a child. The years that followed into her adult life were odd in her mind. Margot made her feel uncomfortable at times. She kept reminding herself Margot was family, and she was lonely, she needed family. The loneliness that no one noticed had begun to consume her from within. Margot was talking about attending yet another fashion show and she simply tuned her out as she drank her glass of wine. The wine numbed the pain. She had begun to drink too much, she told herself of late. Adele closed her eyes as her body began to sway. She wanted the pain to stop, to always be numb, to feel nothing, but the nights were so long. She wanted to prolong the day; the night was where Gillian always waited for her. She fought her with a full life during the day but the nights…the nights. She hated herself in the mornings because she always gave in during the night. Her body always woke up with the pains of the physical and the excess that making love to a ghost produced in her. Soon after this thought the glass fell from her hand and she felt Margot's arms come around her.

"It's okay, Adele; I'll put you to bed."

"No, not yet Margot, I don't want the dark yet..."

"I won't leave you alone. I will stay with you," she whispered in Adele's ear as Adele leaned against her for support.

Adele turned her head, stared at Margot, and pushed her away harshly. "I don't need you! I need more wine."

She walked unsteadily back to where the wine bottle was and poured herself a glass to the brim. She brought the rim of the glass to her lips and began to drink it down quickly. When she finished, she put the glass down so hard on the table that it shattered. She stared at her hand and the last thing she saw was blood oozing down her arm and Margot's voice behind her. Blood, there was so much blood, she remembered Gillian again...so much blood.

Adele woke up the next morning with a pounding headache. No different than usual, she told herself. She raised her arm to cover her eyes from the light and felt something rough against her skin. When she pulled her arms away, she saw her bandaged hand. Stretching her fingers apart she cringed from the pain. She sat up slowly in bed and as usual was naked. She didn't even remember how she got that way anymore. Adele walked slowly towards her bathroom and began to run the water in the tub. She leaned against it and closed her eyes. When the tub was filled, she got in it slowly and let the warmth of the hot water comfort her aching body. The knock on the bathroom door got her attention.

"*Entra,*" she said and closed her eyes with the effort of it.

"I thought you might want to know that mother has arrived." Margot poked her head in the bathroom.

"Oh *mio dio!*" voiced Adele with unhidden dislike.

"She is downstairs with Carlo right now." Margot entered the bathroom and stared hungrily at Adele's body as she bathed.

"I don't want gossip, Margot," she said as she raised herself in the tub and looked towards her sister. "Can I count on you for that?"

"Of course, dearest," she said softly.

Adele stared at her for a moment then returned her attention to the sponge close by and began to wash her body. She turned towards Margot as her eyes noticed her bandaged hand again. "What happened?" she asked as she looked from Margot back to her hand.

"You fell…" Margot trailed off.

"I fell?" Adele asked sarcastically.

"What do you want me to say to you? That you fell because you were drunk and cut your hand open, is that what

221

you want me to say to you?" Margot confronted her with the same type of sarcasm.

Adele continued to wash herself with one hand until she felt Margot's hand cover hers and both sets of eyes locked in a power struggle. For a moment, Adele held on tight to the sponge then simply released it.

"Lean forward so that I can scrub your back. We will get you dressed, go downstairs, and take on Mother together," Margot said to her gently and Adele gave her a conspiratorial smirk and leaned forward to allow Margot to scrub her back.

## CHAPTER FOURTEEN

Adele walked into the large drawing room of the villa at the Caravagio Winery. Unlike her home in New York, the room seemed much bigger with its high windows that seemed to bathe the large expanse with a golden light. The furniture was also of a more European style with pastel silks and gold threads. The house itself dated back over a hundred years and it featured open porticos and large verandas with roman arches. The grounds were lush and green and from the house, the vineyards could be seen in their entirety as far as the eye could behold. The house as well as the vineyard had been a part of the Visconti family for several generations. As Adele turned slightly into the room, she noticed her mother turned to face her. Adele raised her chin with an air of superiority. Her mother nodded to her in recognition. Whether Madeline Visconti, her mother, liked it or not, she bowed to Adele acknowledging the power she held not only over her but the family. Adele held the purse strings; her dead husband had seen to that, so Madeline behaved as much as she was able.

Madeline had always resented the idea that in one way or another she had been subservient to the men in her life. From one to the other, she had always had to cajole or beg for money. And now she had to bow to her daughter's generosity, or lack of. She had expected to be set for life when she had met her Italian count, but custom and his will to give his fortune to his blood children had won out. She had counted on his heart not on his love for his offspring. This had also been a betrayal, Madeline told herself, and this had put a permanent wedge between her and her daughter. It was never that she did not love her children, it was that she loved herself more; she was clear about that. Her dependency on money from her children because of Conte Visconti had been a complete surprise to her the day the will was read.

†

*"Please take a seat," the solicitor suggested to Mrs. Visconti, Contessa de Caravagio. Madeline sat down with great poise. She had to control the joy she was feeling inside her. It wasn't that she had had no feelings for her dead*

*husband, Conte Vittorio Visconti de Caravagio, it was that the anticipation of the wealth that she was about to inherit made her head spin with giddiness.*

*Her children by Vittorio Visconti sat to her right, Matteo her son, next to her, and his twin sister Adele next to him. The twins held hands to comfort each other in their grief. It surprised her because Adele always shied away from being touched. She had always been that way as a baby. When Madeline had attempted to show some affection to her youngest daughter, the child had always pushed her away, preferring the affections of the nanny or the old housekeeper. She had taken care of that right away and had the nanny sacked. She was unable to get rid of the housekeeper because Vittorio would not hear of it. He had insisted that she stay as she had been in the family for many years. Madeline had relented and Adele had always resented her for getting rid of her dear nanny, Teresa, who had always been loving towards her. Unlike his twin sister, Matteo had showered his mother with affection, and she had loved him as much as she was capable of.*

†

Margot entered the room and sat to her right and only looked briefly towards her. Lines had to be drawn for Adele's benefit. She would have a private talk with her mother for assurances later in the day.

"Mama, stop being so difficult about this, it's over! She is finally out of our lives, I have seen to that," Margot insisted.

"That *putana* will never be out of our lives and that *bastarda* carries the name!" Madeline's hatred for Catty was not only evident but it appeared to seethe out of her.

"It is something that will not change. Adele would never be parted from her." Margot stated with crossed arms and walked back and forth in the room. "We must fight the battles we can win, Mama!"

"Carlo is the only legitimate heir. He should not have to share anything with that bastarda!"

"Don't let Adele ever hear you call her that, not ever." Margot said as she stopped in front of the window and watched as Adele walked towards the vineyard. "Sometimes we must be patient and abide our time, Mama." She smiled and then turned to look at her mother with a smile of incredible satisfaction.

† 

Adele stared towards the vines of grapes heavy in their perfection; soon it would be harvesting time. Somehow that just didn't hold the satisfaction that she had expected it to. She was deep in thought when a voice brought her back to reality.

"Mama, tell me about Gillian," Carlo asked softly, and he was caught by surprise at the sadness expressed in his mother's eyes.

"There is nothing to tell. Don't worry yourself; it is not for you to worry about," she said wearily.

"How can you say that? We love her, you love her." He finally saw a spark in his mother's eyes. He also noticed how her stance had straightened with sudden anger.

"She does not! It is done, Carlo, it is done!" She could not control the anger in her voice and Carlo took a step back.

"Why are you being this way? You must stop this. We are a family, and you love her!" he insisted. "Talk to me! I have a right to know."

"She doesn't want me, Carlo. She just doesn't want me anymore." As she said this, she seemed to have lost her breath.

"I don't understand, Mama. I see things. I don't understand," he stated gently.

"It's over, *caro mio*. It's over."

"But I see how she ..."

Adele did not allow him to finish. "Enough, Carlo! No more!" She turned and walked away from him.

†

"Why haven't you called me back, Margot!" The voice on the phone insisted.

"I have been busy," she stated in boredom. "You must be patient."

"You said that we would be together."

"I never promised you anything." She had gotten tired of the game she had been playing with him. After all, she didn't need him anymore. But, she had just one more hand to play. "You promised me that you would take care of my happiness and you have not delivered. You just don't love me enough."

"How can you say that? I have done murder for you!"

"But she is still alive!"

"Margot, the damage is done. I can't..." he begged her.

"If you love me, you will finally end it," she stated flatly. "Then, *caro mio,* we will finally be together forever," she purred. "I cannot wait for you to cover my body with yours and...well, we both know what you like, no?" She hung up the phone.

†

He remained on the phone with only the sound of a dial tone. At that moment the enormity of what he had done finally became clear to him.

Giovanni  de Lanpandusa hung up the phone and at that moment the road before him was finally clear. He walked towards a table close by that held a decanter of a rich brown liquid. He had always enjoyed his French brandy. He poured the brandy to the brim of the tumbler, sat down behind his desk, and began to drink it. He brought the half-filled glass up and pressed it to his forehead. He felt lost and empty.

Margot had taken his pride and his reputation as a doctor. No, he finally admitted. He had done that to himself. He had broken his oath to heal rather than destroy. And for what? Clearly, it had been for nothing. It finally hit him that he had been played. She was never going to be with him. And how could he want a woman when the price had been his soul? He finished the glass and poured himself another.

Sometime during the night, he sat down and stared at the phone. Giovanni took a deep breath and picked it up and dialled.

The ringing seemed to take forever until the voice that he needed to hear said, "*Pronto.*"

†

Adele waited for the person on the other side to speak.

"Contessa, I have failed you and myself..." he slurred.

"Giovanni?"

"I have done murder and I beg your forgiveness. I have always served your family. Your late father trusted that I would take care of his family and I have betrayed that."

"Giovanni, speak for God's sake…just speak!" She was losing her patience with him and his drunkenness.

"Gillian… I have done murder Contessa…" he slurred.

"Giovanni…"

"I met Margot a few years ago and I…" he began.

## CHAPTER FIFTEEN

---

"Gillian! *Amore mio,* listen to me please," she begged in desperation.

"Dell...?" Gillian had begun to hear voices and was not sure whether what she heard was real or merely just part of her dreams. She focused on the phone in her hand then brought it up to her ear again.

"*Amore,* listen to me please. Don't take any medications, do you understand? Please, *amore,* you must listen. I didn't know. God, I didn't know! I love you so very much. Please forgive me. Forgive me," Adele cried in horror. "Gillian, are you there?"

Gillian hung up the phone and walked to the balcony with a smile on her face. It didn't matter that it had been a dream she told herself. She had heard Adele. Even now how she longed to hear her voice. She smiled and she curled up in her favourite corner and drifted off to sleep.

†

Adele ran like a woman who had lost her mind. Making calls and giving instructions. The ambulance to pick up Gillian. Reaching out to Candice to make sure that Gillian took no other medications. Calling for a plane to be made ready so that she and the children would fly back to the States immediately. And during all that time she remembered every word, every deed, and every horrible thing that she had done to Gillian. The gates that had held her sanity in place burst open and she could no longer hold all her emotions in check.

Carlo helped her get everything ready for their departure. She explained to him as much as she knew and gave him specific instructions.

"Come with us, Mama, she will need us," he cajoled her as he held Catty on the tarmac.

"You must go. You and Catty must get there before me. I have to stop her, Carlo. I have to stop Margot before she does any more harm to us. This is what I have to do to keep you all safe. Please tell her that I love her more than my life. Now go! You must both go to your other mama." She

232

kissed him, then kissed Catty. "Go." She turned away from them and got in the car ready to take her to retributions.

†

"Margot…it's over," Giovanni said sadly. "I have finally done the right thing. I wanted…I wanted to hear your voice before…"

"What are you rambling on about?" she stated impatiently. "You are really getting tiresome." She inspected the manicure she had had done that day. She was thinking that she didn't like the shade when she heard a loud sound and pulled the phone away from her ear.

"Giovanni?" she asked as she put the phone to her ear again. "Hello?" She again pulled the phone away from her ear and smiled to herself as she placed it back on its mount. One less thing to worry about, she said to herself.

†

"Mama! Where is Margot?" Adele yelled as she shook her mother by the arms.

"Let go of me! Why should I know where she is?" Madeline looked away from her and at that moment Adele realized that her mother had known too.

"You knew, didn't you? You knew what Margot was doing!" she demanded rather than asked.

"Yes, I knew. It is time that you put away this thing that you do with women. And on top of that, breeding with them. What did you think I would do?" Madeline seethed at her.

"Breed? Did you say breed?"

"That abomination child that you had with her. Not of our blood to inherit and to take away from Carlo. Did you think I would allow that to happen?" Madeline faced her daughter and finally Adele was able to see her mother's true nature in its entirety. She had not thought much of Madeline, but she had never truly expected all the venom that seemed to pour out of her.

"The sperm was Matteo's." Adele simply stated and saw the shock register in the face of her mother.

Madeline grabbed the nearest chair and sat herself down. "No, I don't believe you."

"He wanted me to have my own children as I chose if I ever found someone to love."

"The other one?" Madeline finally voiced the horror that now they shared.

"Yes, it would have been a son. My son and you were party to his murder," Adele said softly. The softness in her voice was more frightening than the yelling. Madeline truly began to feel fear as she now stared at her daughter.

"You will never see the light of day. You will not be missed. No one will care. I will be the only one that knows where you are and that is where you will stay and die. I will be your jailer till your last breath." Adele turned around and walked away.

As Adele left the room, four men walked in and Adele could hear her mother yelling for her as she walked away.

"Adele!"

She would imprison her mother and keep her away where she could never ever hurt them again. Madeline would be locked up in a room with her own demons to torment her. Adele didn't care. She was not the same woman she had once been. Whether it was retribution or justice, it didn't seem to matter. It was done and now on to Margot.

Neither Gillian nor her children would ever be safe with Margot on the loose. She had seen to her mother now onto the next viper to be put down. She had already lost her soul, what did another crime hurt. Adele flew out of the villa and headed now for Margot.

†

Margot was in the tasting room of the vineyard when Adele walked in.

"You must taste this one. I think it will be the finest one to the venture. It will launch the winery…" Margot's voice trailed off as she saw how Adele was staring at her. "Is something wrong?"

"Giovanni…" was all Adele said softly.

"Ah…" she said and stared at Adele. "I do love you, you know. That is the one truth in all this."

Adele stared at her, waiting. Ready to pounce, like something wild, and tear her limb from limb. "Love…"

"I have loved you since the moment you offered me that flower you had picked one day with Papa. Well, your Papa anyway, not mine," she stated in an eerie voice. "I noticed you that day. You were the most exquisite thing I had ever seen." She stared at Adele as she continued to speak. "I wanted you from that moment. I waited but then she got in the way."

Adele stared at her as Margot's words intensified the desire for murder within her.

"I slept with that swine for you!" Suddenly Margot accused. "I did disgusting things with him for you!"

"You tried to kill Gillian! You murdered our baby!" Adele screamed.

"Well…so you are updated," Margot said coldly. "Well, I had my fill. At least for a bit, dearest Dell," she purred. "I enjoyed all of you." She smiled.

Adele stared in confusion.

"Did you think that it was Gillian all those nights?" Margot laughed. "It was me, *cara mia*. It was me," she purred.

Adele stared at her till it suddenly hit her. The enormity and the disgust generated by the words landed on her with such force that she swayed, and her body's revulsion made itself known. She could not stop the vomiting or the nausea.

When Adele looked up Margot knew that she had to run.

Adele chased her as Margot ran toward the garage where the cars were kept. Margot got there first and jumped into the first vehicle, a yellow Lamborghini that was the fastest vehicle in the garage, and sped away with Adele in chase. Margot almost hit Adele as she drove out like the demons of hell were chasing her and she knew they were. Adele ran into the garage and jumped into her black Aston Martin and as the engine roared, she sped out in chase of Margot. They drove recklessly and hit fence posts and the rails that kept the vehicles in certain areas from going over the road along the way. Margot saw through her rearview mirror that Adele was gaining on her and floored the pedal. The roaring of the engine kicked into a higher gear. The screeching of the turns became more frequent and there were near misses with other vehicles as well coming on the opposite direction. As Margot took another turn, she saw another vehicle and she lost control along the curve. In the chase, Adele was not able to keep control of her vehicle either, trying not to hit the oncoming vehicle as well. Both vehicles went over the side. They appeared to take flight for what seemed like forever in slow motion, and then the noise as they hit the ground below filled the air. The smoke was seen from the vineyard as the fire reached upward towards the heavens.

All that Adele felt was pain, but in a blur she saw the flames covering all of the Lamborghini and she knew at that moment that Margot was dead. She was trapped in her seat, and she began to have a hard time breathing. She tried moving once more and she felt so much pain that it felt overwhelming. She gulped for air as the smoke from her own vehicle overtook her and oblivion took her to unconsciousness.

The distant sounds of the *carabinieri* filled the area and the road was closed as vehicles began to arrive to attempt to rescue anyone that might have survived such a crash.

# CHAPTER SIXTEEN

A year later and after long periods of time, she began to breathe again. Her injuries had kept her in hospital for months on end. She had suffered multiple internal injuries from the crash and, in one of the early interventions to save her life from a punctured lung, she almost died on the surgeon's table. Her body was broken, and her mind was in an also broken place. As she came in and out of consciousness, she remembered saying she did not want Gillian to know. The reality of what had become their lives was just too much to bear and Adele didn't want to add the burden. She had no idea what life held or meant anymore. She wasn't even sure why breathing was something she wanted to do. The horrors of what she had learned came back to her in moments like photographs and her body reacted with violent retching.

Early on between being in and out of consciousness, she had heard that Margot had died in the crash, and she smiled. She had memories of her childhood come and go and remembered when she had loved her. When Margot was her beautiful older sister who gave her treats and spoiled her.

In those moments of clarity what kept her alive was her rage. She had chased Margot to her death and a part of her deep inside had still felt some kind of love for her older sister. She remembered when they had been young and Margot was her clever, kind older sister and she had loved her. She shook her head and violently became ill over and over again.

She was filled with a sense of uncaring as well. Her mother would be locked away until her last breath as her punishment. No one would ever know or care when she was no longer seen or heard from. This made her question whether she was still human. In the midst of all the horror that they had lived through this was also a choice. She felt no remorse and no pity. She had taken care of her family and now they would be safe, Gillian and her children, she kept telling herself. No one would ever hurt them. That thought alone made her open her eyes.

And as the time passed and her body began to heal slowly, she realized that Adele had died too on that day, not only Margot. Yes, they had done such horrible things to her, but she was no better. There were some truths, like about her mother, that no one would ever know about. What did that make her? Did she want to be close to Gillian or their children? What type of monster would be near them if she was. After all, she had done murder too. And she was not sorry. But, seeing them was all she longed for. She closed her eyes and tears ran to the side of them freely. All she had known for as long as she could remember now were tears. So many tears and so much pain. Her body began to mend slowly but her soul, however with all the horror was not fit to touch those she loved.

†

Time passed and the healing began. With proper medical care, Gillian had slowly almost returned to her old self. Candice still hung on and just watched from the sidelines, waiting for an opportunity she knew would eventually come. The children seemed happy, and they flourished near Gillian. Carlo had begun to visit his mother since she had come back to New York. He and Catty began to visit her regularly after her absence for the last two years. Communication between Gillian and Adele had been through lawyers. Gillian had tried to communicate directly with Adele to discuss the children, but Adele simply did not respond, and an attorney would reach out to address her concerns. Gillian would drop off Catty as in the years past and pick her up after the allotted agreed upon time. This continued with no contact with Adele.

## CHAPTER SEVENTEEN

Gillian walked into the dark room where Catty was. She was told when she arrived to pick up Catty that the child had fallen asleep, and would be in her old bedroom. When Gillian went up the staircase to get her daughter, she had no apprehension as she had done this many times in the past year. She knew that Adele would not be present nor hinder her picking up their daughter. So, when she opened the door and walked in, she immediately went to pick up her little girl and take her home. So as not to frighten Catty, Gillian did not turn on the light and so it was in the darkness that she heard a voice from the past pulling her back into a time that she did not want to remember.

"Hello, Gillian." The oddly somber voice called out to her from another time, a happier time that was no longer in her present.

"Hello, Adele," was her simple response as she turned around slowly. Gillian was surprised that, as she turned to face her, Adele switched off the hallway light and they were both embraced in a darkness of intimacy.

"Why?" Gillian voiced both out of curiosity and fear. She had not quite gotten over the fear even after their status quo agreement. Adele had kept her promise and given her full custody of Catty, and Giancarlo had also taken to living with her. Adele had insisted on a regular visitation schedule with both children and to also never be present at their pickup and drop off. She remembered Adele saying over the telephone that it seemed very civilized to do it this way and very American. Gillian had not known quite whether she had said this in mockery or as coming from something deeper, like the aristocratic disdain she had always displayed for most people.

Since Adele had sent the children back three years before, she had demanded nothing, asked for nothing but her desire to see the children on a regular basis. The only thing she had not budged on was the financial maintenance, that she did not move an inch from, and the desire for constant security she wanted for not only their two children but for Gillian as well. After all that had occurred it was something that Gillian just had not had the strength to fight her on. This arrangement of dropping off and picking up the children had been one that had gone on for quite some time, and not once had Adele broken her word about not being present but tonight. So, it was with surprise that Gillian now stared at the dark figure standing before her, blocking her way to the doorway.

"I never get tired of looking at our daughter when she sleeps," Adele said with melancholy as she took a step closer to the bed where the sleeping child lay. "She reminds me that there is still innocence and beauty in this black and twisted world."

Gillian stood, unable to move, trying to see a face that clearly wanted to remain in the shadows.

"You gave me that," Adele said softly as she turned to face Gillian, still in the darkness, and only visible from light coming in from a curtain that allowed some light to filter into the room. Adele had her back to the light, making it impossible for Gillian to see her clearly.

"Which am I, how do you see me?" Gillian asked softly, afraid of the response to come.

"Don't ask me that, I am trying so hard to be noble..." Adele trailed off with frustration. "And noble I am having a hard time being," she voiced almost in a growl. She took a few steps closer, holding to the bedpost. "I am not the same. I have become something I don't recognize, and I am trying...I am trying so hard right now." Her breathing was audible and menacing.

"Why would you want to hurt me, Dell?"

"Hurt you?" Adele turned brusquely and walked slowly toward the window as Gillian never lost sight of her. She knew Adele was not the woman she had met and loved years before, neither of them were those people anymore. There had been too much pain to ever forget or forgive. But this Adele she didn't know and still feared. So, when Adele turned quickly back and walked toward her, Gillian took a step back in fear.

"We had an agreement..." The words died in Gillian's mouth as she felt Adele close the distance until only inches were between them. "I don't want to fight anymore. I don't have the strength."

"I don't know what I want...I don't know what or who I am anymore."

Adele spoke in a voice that Gillian did not recognize. Gillian felt her travel from emotion to emotion, unable to stabilize herself as she went from softness to barely manageable anger.

"I don't understand..."

"I hate her so much that I can taste the bile in my mouth with the mere thought of her." Adele's anger appeared barely controlled as she said the words out loud. "It's done. It's finished."

"What are you talking about?" Gillian began to lose her patience. "I just want to collect Catty and go. Let me go."

"I don't want…" Adele whispered as she took a few steps and pulled Gillian roughly to her.

"No," was all that Gillian said.

Adele was barely a breath away and Gillian was unable to move with fear of the monster in front of her.

"You promised to never hurt me again."

"I have done many things, even some that I will go to hell for. But hurting you…no, I don't want to hurt you," she said seductively. "I have watched you every time you come and take my children to live with you and that woman." Adele growled. "I have watched you and I sit here waiting till the time that you come back, again and again. Do you fathom the enormity of that?"

"You said you would let me go, Dell," Gillian reminded her.

"I am not asking for permission; you are my wife!" Adele seemed to surprise herself with her own anger and despair. She took a step back and took in a deep breath before speaking again. "I want to be noble, Gillian. I know the horrors that I have committed and the pain that I have caused. But it doesn't take away the wanting," she finished saying in a whisper of sadness.

Adele was so close that Gillian could feel her breath on her face as Adele once again got closer to her. Gillian felt the fire that emanated from Adele as their bodies were separate but still so close. "Let me go," Gillian whispered in a plea.

"I am trying. What I have learned these last years is that I have not changed. I am still angry and getting angrier. I want to tear things apart and...I am trying to be noble with you but the darkness in me is stronger than all else I feel. You are the only thing that keeps me sane and drives me to madness!" Adele's arms felt like iron grips around her.

"Let me go!" Gillian demanded.

"I can't..." Adele whispered close to her ear. "It is stronger than I am...it always has been." Adele's lips brushed the side of her face, and a groan of pleasure escaped her.

"Let me go!"

"No!" And Adele found her mouth and kissed her as if every fiber of her being needed the kiss to exist.

Gillian pushed her away hard and took a few steps away from her, and as she turned so did Adele. The light of the window illuminated her features and Adele realized what had happened and what it meant with Gillian's intake of breath.

The space between them suddenly became an ocean as Adele turned her face away. The silence between them became a new wall that shot up to the heavens and was just as unbreachable.

"Go! Take her but bring her back as agreed."

"Dell..." Gillian took a few steps closer and pulled at Adele's arm to turn her towards her.

When Adele turned, the scars on her face were suddenly visible with the dim light coming into the room. Gillian reached out to touch her face and for a moment Adele had stood still, but then suddenly pulled her arm away and turned to face Gillian head on.

"This is the monster that lay with you, that almost killed you. The one capable of all the horrors you can imagine and the one who killed our child. Because it was me. It has always been me. This thing inside me that destroys and yet all that I feel is lust...lust is what I feel." Adele grabbed her hard and pulled her against it. "Look at me! This is who I am. This is the thing that wants you, that wants to touch you, taste you, and that needs to be inside you more than it needs air to breathe. I am filled with nightmares Gillian. They don't let me breathe...I am so lost. I need you, *amore.*"

For a moment all that could be heard was ragged breathing as Gillian felt herself being pulled closer towards Adele's body. And Gillian's body began to shake as she felt Adele's lips brush her skin.

"Gillian, don't fear me anymore," she pleaded as her lips sought Gillian's lips with such tenderness that they felt like a flutter on Gillian's lips.

"Mama?"

Upon hearing her daughter, Adele immediately released Gillian, slowly her head turned away once more into the shadows. Adele walked slowly towards the door, leaving the room, as if nothing had transpired between them.

†

Carlo was visiting from school and Gillian had made sure that his favourite chicken cacciatore was made for him. When they sat down for dinner, and he saw what was on the menu he smiled at her as he began to eat it with gusto.

"Why didn't you tell me, Carlo?" she asked him.

Carlo turned towards her and stopped eating with his fork midway. He knew exactly what Gillian was asking him. His gaze suddenly got sad and as his eyes came up to meet Gillian's she could see that he was debating telling her all. He put his fork down slowly onto his plate.

"Please?" she asked him softly as she sat next to him.

"I don't really know everything; I just heard some things…" he trailed off.

"Please…"

"You saw her then?"

Gillian nodded.

"She doesn't really let anyone see her. I asked her once…I think she is in pain most of the time. She suffered internal injuries and almost died on the operating table once. The scars on her face shocked her, I think, and then she just removed herself from people. She broke her arm and leg from the accident too." Carlo looked up as he heard Gillian's intake of breath, but he continued with a need to reveal all that he had been holding inside himself. "She's angry all the

250

time and yells at everyone at the house. Sometimes she really scares me. She won't have any more surgeries, I heard them say, and I don't know why." He finished telling her sadly. "She is only ever patient with me and Catty. But I hear her with other people and it's like she is two people. I don't know all the details. She won't tell me."

"When did it happen, the accident, I mean?"

"After she sent us back here to you. I don't know any more than that."

Gillian shook her head trying to understand and to remember. She could remember the conversation she had had with Adele.

*"Gillian? Gillian answer me!"* Adele was desperately yelling on the other end of the phone. *"Gillian, I need you to listen to me, amore mio, please tell me that you are listening, please."*

*As if from a haze Gillian heard her. She had been getting weaker by the minute and she was barely able to function anymore. Adele's voice was like a beacon that had always been able to reach her. "Dell…"*

*"Amore mio, listen to me. Don't take any more of those medicines that Doctor de Lanpandusa has given you. I have sent an ambulance to take you to the hospital, amore." Gillian could hear the sobs coming from Adele and in her confusion she replied.*

*"Don't cry…"*

251

*"Listen to me, tesoro, I will make this right. I will make this right. The children are on a plane on their way to you and I will make this right; I promise you. Ti amo, ti amo amore."* And with those words the line went dead.

"I don't understand, and I am not sure how to help her," Carlo stated in frustration as he stood up. "I should be able to help her. I need to. She has no one else, Gillian, no one," he said sadly then looked away quickly.

Gillian stood up and took him into her arms. At first, he stood firmly but after a moment he just allowed his arms to go up and clung to Gillian as he wept. "I don't know how to help her. She won't talk to me."

# CHAPTER EIGHTEEN

After her conversation with Carlo, the next time Gillian went to pick up Catty, Gillian did not hear, never mind see, Adele again. Everything after that had gone through Adele's attorneys once more. Every time she would pick up the children, Adele had not been present. And after that night she had begun to think about Adele and wonder how things had ever become this horrible or what had truly happened. Once in a while Carlo would come back visibly shaken after visiting his mother and many times Gillian had tried to talk to him about it, but he had become as secretive as Adele was, and this worried Gillian. Gillian had not been able to erase either the words or the sight of that night when she had last seen Adele after so long. Adele had begun yet again to seep into her thoughts. Candice was always there, always kind, present and patient with her.

When Adele had not called to speak to the children in over a month, Gillian began to worry.

"When are we finally going to be rid of her?" Candice asked, unable to control the ire behind the words.

"Why are you being this way?" Gillian asked in confusion.

"Because we are talking about her. Why can't she just disappear?" Candice growled in frustration. "Gillian, she is getting back into our lives once more, even in her absence. Why are we still doing this?"

Gillian stared at her in shock and just walked away, but before she got to the door to leave the room, she turned around to face Candice.

"Because she is Catty's and Carlo's mother. That is why we will always have to talk about her." After saying that, she left the room and left Candice standing alone staring at the door in disbelief.

Candice sat down on the sofa closest to her and began to accept the notion that Adele would always hold a place that she would never be able to replace. It had been over three years that their world had taken yet another turn after they had learned what Dr. de Lanpandusa had done and how the plot between him and Margot had been discovered. Gillian was healthier and getting stronger by the day. They, however, had not moved forward as a couple. Candice had tried many times to initiate an intimate relationship, but Gillian had asked her for more time. Adele, even now, after all that had transpired, was still standing between them. Candice began to understand that Adele would always hold a place that would separate them forever. She was surprised when she heard a door close to the side of her. When Candice looked up, she saw Carlo standing there, staring at her.

"You don't have to like my mother, but you will not yell at Gillian because of her," he stated firmly. "I will not allow you to speak to her that way, do you understand?"

"Don't talk to me that way, Carlo. You and I don't have to go down this route".

"I will say what I want to you when I see you yell at her."

"This is none of your concern."

"Gillian is my concern, and she always will be. Whether you like it or not, whether you like me or not. She is a Visconti," he challenged her.

"Yes, I can see your mother in you."

"Thank you."

"It was not a compliment."

"We both know where we stand then. You don't have to stay. After All, this is my mother's house, as we both know," Carlo stated arrogantly then turned around and left the room.

Candice felt utterly defeated. She shook her head, telling herself repeatedly how foolish she had just been. And in that moment, she began to ask herself how long she could stand living this way.

When Adele had agreed to the separation, she had been ecstatically happy. Adele had given Gillian custody of the children but had insisted on having a say in where they lived, where they would go to school, and the security. The allowance that was deposited monthly into Gillian's bank account was, at the very least, obscene. Candice had accepted the idea because she saw it as an end, but she now realized that it would never end. Everywhere she looked, Adele was there. Carlo was right, they lived in her house, surrounded by her things, the art pieces on the wall, the artifacts that she and Gillian had collected when they lived together, and her children. They would always be her children, Adele and Gillian's, never even slightly hers. Catty began to look more like Adele every day and, although Gillian was visible there, too, it only reminded Candice of their union. Rather than seeing Catty as Gillian's, and Gillian's alone, the child was a testament of the union of Gillian and Adele more and more each day. And now she had made an enemy of Carlo.

# CHAPTER NINETEEN

---

Gillian was, yet again, leaving Adele a message on her private line, and again, was faced with the frustration of not knowing what was going on. A few days later when her cell phone rang, she immediately answered it, breathlessly.

"Dell, I have been calling you for weeks!" She took a deep breath before she continued, "This is not what we agreed to, Dell. If you can't see the children, you have to let me know. You were adamant about the schedule and then you disappear. Did it occur to you that Carlo and Catty might wonder why you just fell off the earth, as you put it?"

Gillian waited for an answer and when she heard nothing, she got mad all over again. "Dell!"

"I'm sorry, it could not be helped," Adele answered softly.

The silence grew between them and something inside Gillian began to worry. "What's wrong, Dell?"

"Nothing is wrong. Everything is now very right." She answered with such softness that Gillian's intake of breath could be heard by Candice sitting on the other side of the room.

"Where are you?" Gillian pleaded.

"I won't be able to see the children for a while. Business calls, you know. Please tell them that I love them each and every day, *amore*. I have to go now, my plane is waiting," Adele finished, her voice barely audible to Gillian. "I am giving you what you have been begging me for... peace, *amore*."

Candice stood behind her now, listening, waiting.

All that Gillian knew was that she wanted to keep Adele on the phone for some insane reason that only her heart understood. "Wait..."

"I can't, *amore*. I must go," Adele said softly. "Gillian..."

"Yes..."

"I...I just wanted..." she trailed off.

"I can't do this now, Dell." Gillian felt Candice standing behind her and was confused by Adele's behaviour. "No games, we agreed. When can I tell the children that they will see you?"

Gillian heard someone in the background say, "It's time, Contessa."

"Yes…" Adele responded. "Goodbye, Gillian."

The line went dead, and Gillian stared at it as fear began to grow inside her. She redialled over and over again, but the call kept going into voicemail repeatedly.

She left Candice standing in surprise as she went looking for Carlo.

Gillian finally found Carlo with Catty. He looked up as soon as he saw Gillian enter the room.

"Have you heard from your mother?" She was unable to hide her concern as she spoke to him.

"Yes, she wanted to speak to me and Catty. That's why I am here with Catty now." He found it hard to hide his semblance from Gillian.

†

Adele flew back to Italy and focused on her winery. Afterall, she told herself, she had almost run it to the ground with neglect. She had done the right thing by Gillian. She checked on Gillian and their children daily with those invisible to them. She needed to know that they were safe. She knew that Candice might object but she needed the peace of mind. Her world, she realized, was a dark place. She trusted no one and no one would ever get close enough to

259

hurt her family ever again. All she loved she needed to protect, to watch over even if they didn't see the need for it.

She spoke with Carlo and Catty almost daily, but she desperately missed being able to touch them. There were things that needed her attention and she could not afford to be weak. Not anymore. Her heart had gotten cold in the past few years and the white that covered her temples was but a sign of how the cold grew within her. Gillian and their children would soften her, and she could not take a chance on it.

Finally, it was over. Adele closed her eyes as her mother's casket was lowered to the grown without pageantry. It was over, it was finally over, and all that it had cost her was her soul. She wore the scars on her face to remind her just how high the cost was.

†

"Gillian, I need you to agree to this!" Candice demanded.

"I am not saying that I won't go, I am saying that I can't next Thursday. Catty has ballet lessons that day at the same time, Candice." Gillian tried to keep calm.

"You knew last week when we made this appointment."

"They changed the lesson because of the upcoming show. I didn't know until today." Gillian tried to explain to Candice, but it only seemed to agitate her.

"And it's more important than our going to see Doctor Cambridge?" Candice turned away from her and walked towards the window, trying to control the growing anger inside her. "At the end of the day, everything is more important than me."

"That's not true…" Gillian said barely above a whisper.

Candice turned to face her. "Yes, it is."

"I want to make this work, Candy, honestly."

"You never have time, Gillian. It's always something. This is a chance for us to work on us, not the children, not anything but you and me. We agreed!" Candice felt the anger rising again.

"I wouldn't have agreed to go and speak to a counsellor if I didn't want to try and make things work with us." Gillian touched Candice's arm and caressed it up and down.

Candice looked down and closed her eyes, wanting to believe her, but almost just as quickly walked away, putting down distance between her and Gillian.

"I honestly thought that she would be gone by now, but she is still here. Another year, but she is still here." She stared at Gillian, waiting for a response.

261

Gillian said nothing and sat down on the nearest chair in the plush, grand room. And suddenly something made her look around all the things that Candice saw. The paintings on the walls, the artifacts, the chair she was sitting at. She caressed the arm of it, remembering how she and Adele had playfully argued over the colour.

Candice looked around in frustration. "She is in everything!"

Gillian continued to say nothing, looking away, still silent.

"You aren't even arguing the point anymore."

"I am tired of responding to this accusation," Gillian responded wearily.

"Because it's true!" Candice raised her voice in frustration. She took a few steps away then, just as quickly, turned around and continued yelling, "She is in this damn floating palace, in this city, in every place we go to!"

"Have you lost your mind?" Gillian stared at her in disbelief. "In the city and every place?"

"Yes, Gillian. Everywhere I turn she is there mocking me. I can't even touch you without you reacting. Don't you think I know why?" Candice realized that she was losing control.

"I agreed to go to the damned counsellor, didn't I?"

"She dragged you to hell!"

"I chose to go!"

They stood facing each other, knowing that too much had been said between them and that some truth had been uncovered.

"Yes, you did, didn't you?" Candice said softly, turned around, and walked out of the room, leaving Gillian finally needing to consider what her words meant not only to Candice but to herself.

Gillian walked to the large window that overlooked the park and she realized that she could not move forward until she dealt with her past. Finally, she had accepted that realization. Every road not taken would have led her to this, but she had chosen repeatedly to not see it. Perhaps it was she who was more herself each and every day, or maybe it was that she was finally ready to see what she wanted her future to truly be. Because, through it all, at the end there had always been Adele. Even after all the horror there was Adele looking back at her. She needed to finish all ties so that her future had a chance of going anywhere. She got up, picked up the phone and dialled in anticipation.

"Hello?"

# CHAPTER TWENTY

---

Adele did not take her calls, but the lawyers got back to her. Her demands had been made clear; she would only speak to Adele. Her telephone rang within the hour.

"Are the children alright?" A worried voice came through the receiver and Gillian took a deep breath for the first time in a long while, which kept her silent.

"Are the children alright, Gillian?" Adele asked with growing concern.

"The children are fine," Gillian said simply.

"What do you want?"

"We have to talk…"

"We have nothing to talk about. I gave you what you asked me for." Adele's voice began to grow irate.

"I am not free. I need clarity so that I can move forward, otherwise I am still a prisoner," Gillian demanded.

The silence felt tangible between them.

"What do you want, Gillian?" Adele asked gently this time.

"I need to be free so that I can find some type of peace. I can't seem to move forward. I can't breathe," Gillian said close to tears.

"Don't cry, please," Adele responded softly. "You wish to be completely free of me, yes?" It took everything in her to say the words.

"Come to New York. I need to see you, to talk to you. This has to end. Whatever this is between us must end."

"It's almost April. I will meet you by the Jefferson Memorial. It's only right that this end where it began. I will let you know the time and date." With this the line went dead and Gillian slowly put down the receiver.

✝

"You have got to be kidding me!" Candice ranted. "You are not going!"

"Excuse me?"

"No, enough is enough. When will this end?" Candice took a deep breath before continuing with the tirade. "No wait, it will never end, will it?"

Both stood at a stand-off then suddenly Candice just visibly began to show the signs of stress in her semblance. "Why don't we just talk about the elephant in the room?"

Gillian remained silent.

"I don't know if it's her or not. What I do know is that it's not me." She just sat down looking at the carpet. Gillian sat next to her not affirming or denying the words.

"Who are we fooling. It's always been her. No matter what she has done, it's always been her."

"I need to talk to her in person, Candice. There is simply too much to clear up and a phone will just not do," Gillian said gently.

Candice suddenly stood up, towering over her. "I would simply have more respect for you if you just told me the truth!"

"What would that be, Candice?" Gillian tried to be patient.

"That you are still in love with her!" She took a few steps away from Gillian before turning to face her again. "Both of you just can't seem to stop yourselves. Jesus Christ!" she finished saying as she ran her fingers through her hair in exasperation. "I can't do this anymore." She turned towards the door and walked out of the room, leaving Gillian speechless.

Candice came face to face with Carlo and stopped abruptly. "Well, you won't have to see me anymore, Carlo. I know you will be glad to see me go."

"I never disliked you," he said earnestly which took Candice by surprise.

"I will miss you."

"Are you leaving?"

"I was never truly here. I just didn't see it," she answered sadly. "As you told me once; this is your mother's house."

"And Gillian is my mother's wife," he said arrogantly.

"Yes, yes, she is." Candice walked away to try to decide what to do next. Her life for the last few years had been consumed by Gillian. She now had to figure out how to live without her. A part of her had always known that this moment would come, she just had not wanted to accept the inevitable. She had never stood a chance. She should have seen it but she hadn't wanted to and, no matter what the cost, she would have done it again if she thought there was the smallest chance.

# CHAPTER TWENTY-ONE

Gillian did receive information from Adele's lawyer as to dates and times and, once all the details were worked out, she accepted the private jet that Adele had sent to take her to D.C. When she got off the plane, she felt a rush of soft warm air caress her skin. It was early April, but it was deliciously warm. And Gillian went to meet Adele, as agreed upon, at the Jefferson Memorial.

When Gillian arrived, she did not see Adele at first, until she recognized a dark-clad figure. She was down the path surrounded by the pink cherry blossoms that floated softly in the breeze like tiny pink ballerinas. She walked slowly towards Adele and, almost by an invisible pull, Adele turned, and their eyes met.

They stood in front of each other, unable to speak, just basking in the nearness until Adele broke the spell by turning away. "Thank you for meeting me here," she said softly.

"I need to know the whole truth."

"The truth…"

"Yes, everything. I want to know everything so that I don't have to imagine any more horror." Gillian pulled at Adele's arm to face her.

Adele looked at her and without any emotion told her what she needed to hear. "No one will get close to you and the children again."

"Why can't you just tell me the truth?"

Adele turned away from her. "The truth is that you thought I was harsh, but I wasn't harsh enough. The truth is that my sister Margot orchestrated killing you with Dr de Lanpandusa. She drove him to suicide, and I chased her to her death in a car. The truth is that once I loved her when she was just my big, beautiful sister. I don't know what happened to her but something inside her was rotten. The truth is that she drugged me and raped me, night after night. The truth is that I drove her to her death, and I haven't felt clean since then." She suddenly turned around and grabbed Gillian by both arms as she continued, "The truth is that I chased my mother and, when I found her, I locked her up until she died of a stroke, alone, because I couldn't trust that she wouldn't come after you and our children again." She released Gillian and took a few steps away towards the rail close by. Then she continued softly, "The truth is that I am broken and that I am just as scarred on the inside as my face is where the world can see. I am a monster. I don't want to be your monster, *amore*." She finished barely audibly in her pain.

The confession left Gillian reeling. Words failed her and the silence became unbearable.

"We are both broken now." Adele's voice was shaky. "I have broken the most beautiful thing in my life. I am drowning in the nightmares…"

Gillian wanted to comfort her, but there was so much pain and anger in the past between them that the bridge to make that happen just didn't exist. "I'm so sorry," were all the words that Gillian was able to mutter.

"Can you ever forgive me?" Adele could not control the pain in her voice as she said the words. She could still not face Gillian.

The silence said it all.

"I will have the divorce papers drawn up and sent to you," she said finally as she turned to face Gillian and raised her chin arrogantly.

"Thank you."

"Goodbye, Gillian." She tried to sound detached but the tear that escaped and rolled down her cheek reached Gillian more than words could. "Perhaps, in another life, I would simply say I will wait here for you every spring and trust that one day you will come back to me."

Gillian watched her walk away and something inside her cut at her heart once more. They had loved so deeply but the violence and the horrors that separated them were so difficult to comprehend and forgive. And yet, it hurt to watch Adele walk away from her.

# CHAPTER TWENTY-TWO

The divorce papers arrived but, somehow, the right time to sign them never seemed to come. Adele had begun to see the children again but had kept her word and did not try to see Gillian again. Candice moved out a few months later. Somehow details were finally taken care of and many other things put to rest. Mostly time had healed many wounds and made forgiveness of many injuries perhaps possible.

Carlo came into the grand room and found Gillian deep in thought. He had walked up to her, calling her by name, and she had not heard him. It was only when he touched her arm that she turned towards him slowly. She stared at him and smiled.

"What are you smiling about?"

"You have gotten so tall. I miss the little boy I guess," she said sadly.

"You are being so silly!" He laughed.

"Yes, yes, I am. Have I told you how proud of you I am lately?"

"Yes, at least a zillion times."

"Good."

"What were you thinking about anyway?"

"Your mom."

"I ..." He wanted to say so much but he also knew that there were things that they had to work out on their own.

"How is she?"

"Moody as Mom always is but not with me or Catty." He took a deep breath and said what he longed to say to her. "I miss when we were a family."

Gillian looked deeply into his eyes searching for something. "Do you?"

"Yes, yes, I do. Very much." He kissed her on the cheek and left her to her thoughts.

Gillian looked out the window again and in the silence she smiled.

†

It was spring again and the cherry blossoms once again were floating through the breeze. It was a quarter past one in the afternoon in early April, and the breeze was warm as Gillian walked along the river, close to the Jefferson Memorial. She smiled as she saw a woman with dark hair in the distance. The closer she got to the figure in the distance, her heart began to beat faster and faster, to the point that she could feel the pounding in her ears. When she was only a few feet away, the figure spoke but had not turned to face her.

"I have waited for you my whole life…I don't have the words. I am afraid. I don't have anything to offer you but the pieces that are left of me, and I don't know if that is enough or if you will ever forgive me." Adele finally turned to face her. Tears filled her eyes waiting for the words that she had no hope would come.

"I love you," Gillian said the words. She reached out and caressed the arrogant Contessa's face. The scars were there but the softness in her eyes was there too. Gillian took the Contessa by the hand. "I am glad you waited."

Gillian softly kissed her Contessa's lips as the warm breeze whirled around them with the pink swirls of cherry blossoms.

"*Amore…*" whispered Adele and wept.

†

"Carlo! You moved the piece six times not five," Catty scolded her big brother.

Carlo laughed out loud. "Did not"

"You did too! You are cheating!" Catty continued to argue with her brother.

"Okay, okay, should I throw the dice again?" he asked innocently.

"In your deepest dreams, you already moved. Only five moves, Carlo." Catty was staring at her brother when she realized he had been playing with her. She picked up the piece of the board game and threw it at him playfully. Both began to laugh as they threw the pieces of the board game at each other.

At that moment the door opened, and both looked towards its direction. Carlo and Catty both simultaneously yelled in both surprise and joy, "Mama!"

Adele and Gillian opened their arms as their children filled their embrace.


The End

# Epilogue

---

*The love that at times survives in the ashes. There is always hope in the embers.*

## ABOUT THE AUTHOR

---

<u>S Anne Gardner</u> With a vast array of varied life experiences S. Anne has a wide array of story ideas that she often weaves into riveting storylines that takes the reader on some unexpected rides. She has lived all over the world and is now permanently living on the East Coast of the United States although she does still like to travel. She has a love that fills her heart and children who fill her life. She works in the field of finance and is a published author. Her published works include *Por Amor, For the Love of a Woman, An Affair of Love* and *Compensation.* She enjoys sailing, horseback riding, art, traveling, reading, and writing. Her family, her friends, and her music fill her life in a world that is her own.

Email: <u>sanneol7@aol.com</u>

## OTHER AFFINITY BOOKS

---

<u>The Sky People by Ali Spooner</u>
After a beautiful wedding, Eli and Whit return to plan the next phase of their relationship. Whit discovers the identity of her father, and he shares a future with her that will change life on Cast Iron Farm forever. Twins bless the Fortner family, and Eli shares a special secret with Mitch, who bonds with the children in a unique way. Ride along as the Fortners begin a new chapter of their story.

<u>Love Bonds by Annette Mori</u>
When Mila Thompson, a rookie police officer, discovers her mother is missing, she engages the assistance of San Diego's number one detective, who is more than a

little reluctant to enter the fray, noting she works in homicide, not missing persons.

Bernie doesn't play well with others, which is why she doesn't have a partner at work or in her personal life. When Mila approaches her, she tries hard to refuse the request, but Mila will not accept no for an answer. For reasons she does not understand, Bernie doesn't want to say no to Mila, who can charm her way into anything, including smoothing the rough edges of Bernie's crusty heart.

Things get complicated when the women in The Organization have an unusual tie to Mila's mother. This sets up an action-packed adventure with twists and turns and a healthy dose of love. Find out the future of The Organization and whether an unlikely pair can find their way to love.

Holy Water and Whiskey Scars by Ali Spooner
Faith Wilson and Logan Bronson have family secrets to protect and a legacy to uphold to support their small rural Appalachian community. Their commitment to each other is strong, and their desire to aid the struggling families however they can, lead them both down an exciting but dangerous path. Will their love continue to grow and be the glue that binds the community together, or will they flee the withering community?

Politics of Love by Annette Mori

Governor Sandra Murphy is rethinking the sanity of allowing her mother to talk her into considering becoming the democratic party's choice for the presidential nominee. Sandra has enough to contend with after surviving a bomb attack, thanks to the brave border control agent working alongside the clever undercover FBI agent. Now she has to worry about a pesky reporter who seems to be everywhere scoping stories Sandra would prefer Wynter Holmes steer far away from.

Wynter admires the charismatic governor. After all, she voted for the woman. But that doesn't give Governor Murphy a free pass. A breaking story is what Wynter lives for, and she isn't about to stop digging just because the engaging governor is attractive, single, and an out lesbian. Reporting for the famously biased, right-wing media conglomerate is not exactly making Wynter a friend of the enigmatic leader.

Will repeated attempts on Governor Murphy's life where Wynter might be collateral damage bring them closer together or tear them apart from what might be a perfect match?

Out and Loud by Ali Spooner

The Bentleys have begun celebrating their success by performing live in small venues and outdoor concerts. Their music and love for one another continue to grow as their number drops to four. Stone is needed at home to run the business during his father's rehabilitation, but the Bentleys drive forward. Cedra's challenge to her bandmates to create original songs for their next album turns into brilliant love songs, rockabilly, and a Pride Festival anthem. Ride along with the Bentleys as they capture the hearts of country music lovers across the nation.

<u>Undercover Love</u> by Annette Mori

When the domestic terrorist cell Emma Schmidt has infiltrated summons her to an abandoned warehouse for a loyalty test, Emma immediately recognizes the battered woman. Emma must act fast to protect her cover and save the woman, Jimena Aguilar, she's never forgotten.

Emma and Jimena team up on a dangerous mission to take down the terrorist cell and save the life of the popular California governor.

Will this lead them back to the closeness they once shared or have the years in between hardened their hearts to love.

<u>Changing Times</u> by Jen Silver

Thirty years on from when we first met Dani Barker and Camila Callaghan in *Changing Perspectives*, they're enjoying marriage and semi-retirement in a luxury flat near London.

Dani's niece, Holly, runs their mixed media business, now gaining a foothold in the highly competitive online games market. Holly's older sibling, Luc, influences people to take action on climate issues with their website, Gaia One: One Earth, One Chance.

Romance has been in short supply for both Holly and Luc. Immersed in her work, Holly's dating life is non-existent. For Luc, family prejudices stand in the way of a relationship with the love of their life.

Can Holly and Luc succeed in making the changes necessary to achieve their own happy ever afters?

Midnight in Nashville by Ali Spooner

The Bentleys have successfully finished cutting their first album, *Six Strings, and a Dream.* When the Covid-19 epidemic hits, tours and live performances are cancelled as the world goes into lockdown. With the closing of the restaurant, employment for the band members has been severely impacted. The group comes together to make life work at Ma Bentley's Boarding House. They take advantage of their down time and use of the studio to record more songs. Cedra has challenged each of her bandmates to create a song for their next album. Juliet's song, "Midnight in Nashville," is chosen as the title track. Join the group as they venture into new marketing avenues and create their first music video for the title track.

Compound Interest by Annette Mori

The kick-ass women in The Organization are back and they have their sights set on a few new recruits. Not everyone is jumping for joy at the choices, considering subterfuge is front and center in the games the new recruits have been playing.

Dani is supposed to get her happily ever after, but she's not sure what's real anymore including Candy's feelings for her. When a new enemy takes Candy captive, Dani vows to uncover the truth by insisting on going on the mission to save her. Candy is not what she seems, and that presents a new set of complications for Dani and her feelings.

The Organization continues to have challenges when those damn book magicians and book witches keep popping back in to warn them of new catastrophes on the horizon. She doesn't have time for their warnings, until their enemies intersect once again to keep them working together.

From award-winning author, Annette Mori, find out what happens in this final chapter of the combined Asset Management/Book Addict series.

Six Strings and a Dream by Ali Spooner

Cedra Tyler's dream of becoming a songwriter in Nashville was put on hold due to her mother's failing health. When the time came for Cedra to start her journey, she left her home in south Alabama with a heavy heart.

Arriving at Ma Bentley's boarding house, meeting her housemates, also fledgling musicians, she feels the warmth she was missing since leaving home.

Her housemates realize Cedra's talent as a song writer and begin to gel as a group. The pain and loss she had experienced added a layer of emotion and longing in her lyrics unusual for someone of her age.

They form a band, The Bentley's, named after Ma who is much more than a landlord to them all. Cedra falls for bandmate Juliet, and that inspires her creativity even more.

Will The Bentley's achieve their dream of making it big in Music City? Has Cedra found her forever in the arms of Juliet?

Affinity
Rainbow Publications

eBooks, Print, Free eBooks

Visit our website for more publications available online.

www.affinityebooks.com

Published by Affinity Rainbow Publications
A Division of Affinity eBook Press NZ LTD
Canterbury, New Zealand

Registered Company 2517228